The Talking Stick

Volume 9

A Literary Cookbook Issue

Original Works by Minnesota Writers & Artists

A Publication of the Jackpine Writers' Bloc and Friends

Editor: Bonnie Louther
Art Editor: Dawn Rossbach
Project Director: Carolyn Spangler
Layout and Production: Dawn Rossbach
Gail Gardner
Shannon Geisen
Business Sponsorship: Florence Witkop
Vivian Sazama
Publicity: Shannon Geisen
Marketing: Janet Pratt
Betty Sayers
Copy Editors: Bruce Bolton
Julia Logermeier
Editorial Board: Cathy Connell
Sandy VanCampen
Mary Wiley
Aurora Clark

ISBN: 1-928690-01-7

This publication is made possible in part, by a grant from Region 2 Arts Council- McKnight Grant.

dedicated to

Linda Henry

who gave birth to the Talking Stick.
It is with her love, passion, and inspiration,
that her children carry on.

Table of Contents

Table of Contents

Index of Recipes

Bonnie Louther

Editor's Note

Almond and Anisette Biscotti

2 cups all purpose flour
1 tablespoon grated lemon peel
1 tablespoon instant espresso powder
or instant coffee powder
2 1/2 teaspoons baking powder
1 teaspoons aniseed, finely chopped
1 teaspoons salt
1/2 cup (1 stick) chilled butter, cut
into 1/2" pieces
1 1/2 cups sliced almonds
1 cups sugar
2 eggs
1/4 cup anisette (anise-flavored
liqueur)

Preheat oven to 350 degrees. Butter and flour cookie sheet or sheets. Mix first 6 ingredients in large bowl. Add butter and cut in until mixture resembles coarse meal. Add nuts and sugar. Mix eggs and anisette in small bowl. Add to dry ingredients and mix until dough forms. Divide dough into 3 pieces. Gently knead each piece to bind. Form each into 1 1/2" wide log. Transfer to prepared pans. Bake until golden brown and firm to the touch, about 35 minutes. Cool in pan on rack for 15 min. Using serrated knife, cut logs into 3/4" thick slices, at an angle. Arrange cut side up on cookie sheet at same temperature. Bake until golden brown about 10-15 minutes on each cut side. Cool on rack. Store in airtight container.

Food not only is a necessity in our lives, but it also invokes feelings of peacefulness, comradeship, love and well being.

I believe cooking is an art form. Mixing ingredients and serving a tasty meal is very similar to an artist blending paints from his palette to create a painting, or a musician putting notes together to create a melody.

The comradeship involved with sharing a meal with those you love has been an important part of our family life for many years. Gathering around the kitchen table for our evening meal was one time in our busy day when everyone was present. We encouraged discussions about activities at school, and the events of the day and world concerns. We urged our children to participate with their ideas, no matter how different they were from their siblings'. However, we followed strict rules for etiquette at the table and our children learned at a very early age how to pass a serving dish, to keep their elbows off the table, to respect the person that was talking and allow each person to have their say. These same principles are behind the philosophy of The Talking Stick.

The Jackpine Writers' Bloc has talked about publishing a "Literary Cook Book" for over two years. We have finally decided that the time was right. Hopefully, you will enjoy our poems, essays and short stories we have included in this issue, as well as some of our favorite tried-and-true recipes from members and friends.

So without further ado, help yourself to your favorite biscotti, pour yourself a cup of coffee and read on.

Bon Appetit!

PUMPKIN
bLOCK PRINT

Kayla Peterson

Marion C. Holtey

Sally's Sweet Potatoes

2 (16 oz.) cans sweet potatoes
1 can apricot halves (save juice)
1/2 cup walnut halves

1/2 cup brown sugar
1 1/2 tablespoons cornstarch
1 teaspoon cinnamon
1 tablespoon butter

Place sweet potatoes in a greased 9x13 pan. Arrange apricot halves and walnuts over potatoes.

Mix brown sugar, cornstarch, and apricot juice in saucepan. Cook until mixture thickens. Add butter and cinnamon, and pour over potato mixture.

Bake at 350 degrees for 30 minutes.

Jacob's Thanksgiving

C an we all go to the beach?" begged the children, as they rushed through the door. The service was over. Friends and neighbors had stopped to visit and offer their condolences. Now only the family remained. "We need to help grandpa prepare dinner," said Aunt Helen.

"Be gone with you," Jacob ordered. "Don't waste precious time. Enjoy the waves, the sunshine and each other. But be back by seven for dinner."

They glanced at one another, then Aunt Helen said, "O.K., but make it simple, don't fuss, Dad."

Jacob tied the tattered apron over his new shirt. He put a disc in the CD player and assembled the food on the kitchen table. Alone at last, his skilled hands sliced, mixed, and stirred to the rhythm of Beethoven's 5th Symphony. Tears that had refused to fall at the funeral service that morning now fell on the onions as he chopped them for the dressing.

Sally's struggle had been long, fierce. Jacob tried to forget the harsh words hurled from the lips of his sweetheart. He knew they were only strange symptoms of the cruel disease that had scrambled her brain. Still, they hurt.

He reached for cinnamon to sprinkle over the sweet potatoes, and felt Sally's fingerprints on the jar. She always made her special casserole for holidays. Jacob smiled as he almost added a third can of potatoes to the dish. He often suggested this, teasing Sally about her Uncle Ted's appetite. Her standard reply was, "He can have a peanut butter sandwich if he's still hungry."

Delicious aromas and *Fur Elise* greeted the family as they returned from the beach. They sat down at the lace-covered table, set exactly as Sally would have arranged it for a special occasion. The sideboard held platters filled with turkey, dressing, salad, cranberries and all the fixings.

Jacob looked around the festive table, bowed his head, and thanked God for their many blessings. He passed the sumptuous platters to his hungry family. Then he raised his fork to taste once more his Sally's sweet potatoes.

$^\text{¢}$HERRY $^\text{s}$WIRL

$^\text{b}$LOCK PRINT

Leah Hanninen

Dessert First

We lived in Madison, Wisconsin, during the late 60's. Riots and anti-Viet Nam war demonstrations were not uncommon on the college campus. We lived in a residential area near campus, and everyday National Guard trucks would pass our home, carrying assault rifles, riot gear and tape on their windows. Drug use was prevalent on campus and even in high school.

I was worried about the older children and needed to stay as close to them as I could because of the hectic times. I gave them articles to read about the use of drugs and what lasting effects it could cause. After they had read the articles, we'd have a family discussion about what they had read and what it meant.

At our evening meals our children were always encouraged to discuss what happened at school that day or anything else that concerned them. With nine children, from 18 to 2 years old, there was a large range in ages. We had talked to the children who were in high school and asked them to come to us if they had any problems. We promised to listen.

One night after the little ones were in bed, the three older children came into the kitchen and said they wanted to talk about something important. My first thought was someone in our family was using drugs, or thinking of joining a cult, or something horrible. My heart raced as I tried to remain calm, and said, "Let's go into the den and we can talk."

The oldest of the boys, Casey, said, "Mom, why don't we have dessert every night? You've told us that fresh fruit, jello and bread pudding is dessert, right? Well, when I was at Jimmy's house the other night for supper, they had banana splits and Jimmy says they have desserts like that every night."

"When I was at Margaret's for supper, her mom made a cherry pie, and it wasn't even anyone's birthday or a holiday," our oldest daughter, Debi, said.

"We had chocolate cake for dessert at Jay's," Scott chimed in. "His dad is even divorced," he added.

I almost wanted to laugh, but merely said, "I'll think this over and let you know. Thank you for coming to me with your problem. Now it's time to go to bed, you have school tomorrow."

I poured myself a cup of coffee, hands shaking from relief, and sat at the kitchen table to ponder the situation.

First of all, if I gave in to them, I would be fixing desserts every night besides the main meal. No, I thought, I can't do that. On their birthdays, they were given a choice of the dinner they wanted, besides a birthday cake and ice cream, and on holidays, we always had dessert. With the number of birthdays we had in a year plus holidays, I decided it was enough sweets for growing boys and girls. Besides, our dental and doctor bills were minimal, and I intended to keep it that way. So, I would have to think of something to satisfy them.

The next day, the three oldest came into the kitchen for an answer. I told them, "Alright, this is what we'll do. Sunday we'll have dessert first, then our evening meal, how's that?"

They looked as if they had won a prize at the state fair. They gave each other a knowing look, and came over to give me a big hug and kiss. "Thanks, mom," they said in unison.

Then on second thought, Casey said, "Can I invite Jimmy?" I told him he could and suggested that Debi invite Margaret and Scott invite Jay for supper.

The next Saturday I baked all day. I made two cherry pies, an apple pie, chocolate cake, brownies and two angel pies, a family favorite. When I bake pies I end up with flour all over myself and most of the kitchen. By the time I had finished baking, the kitchen was a mess. It took me hours to make it presentable.

After church we had a good breakfast and I told them dessert would start at 5 o'clock. There were smiles all around the table.

It seemed a good time to give them one more luxury. They could eat their desserts in the den while they watched the movie "Born Free".

The time had come. I placed all the desserts on the kitchen table and told them to take as much as they wanted. They did and came back for seconds and thirds.

Before the show was over, I started fixing hamburgers for the evening meal. The smell of the cooking hamburgers wafted into the den.

As the movie was coming to a close, Elsa, the young lioness raised by humans, was in the wild stalking her first meal.

One by one they came into the kitchen, only to run out holding their hands over their mouths and groaning. The youngest, Marti, laid her head on my lap, and said, "My tummy hurts." They all went upstairs to their bedrooms. I went upstairs, Alka-Seltzer in hand, only to find them curled up and fast asleep.

Never again did they ask for dessert first.

Angel Pie

4 egg whites
1 cup sugar
1 teaspoon cream tartar
1/2 teaspoon vanilla
a pinch salt

Beat whites until foamy, then add cream of tartar and beat stiff. Add sugar gradually until the consistency of meringue. Add vanilla. Bake in well greased large pyrex pie plate at 275 degrees for 1-1/2 hours. Cool completely before filling.

Filling

1/2 cup sugar
4 egg yolks
Juice of 2 lemons
1 cup whipping cream, whipped

Beat yolks until lemon color, then add sugar and lemon juice. Cook in double boiler for 15-20 minutes until clear and coats spoon. Mixture will thicken as it cools. Remove from heat. Add 1 Tablespoon butter.

Spread 1/2 of whipped cream over cooled pie shell (no vanilla or sugar in whipped cream). Cover with cooled lemon filling and spread remainder of whipped cream over the top.

Cover and refrigerate for 24 hours.

Carson Gardner

Without Looking

You Will Have Great Success,
so intones the fortune-cookie oracle.
I drop cheap rice paper
into cold green tea,
push away moo goo gai pan
and reflect
upon my debts and doubts and hunger,
my failures and outrageous dreams.
Why am I still trying desperately
to grow blue-heron wings,
to find that fudge nirvana,
to win my black belt
at last
in serendipity?
Perhaps I should lose a few pounds
and fantasies,
get a better day job,
stop giving my anonymous heart,
spurn martial arts and chocolate.
Perhaps I should bask in opulent boredom,
that stereotype success.
But I don't type that well,
I can't afford the stereo
and I would never pass
my bored exam.
Perhaps I should—
but I won't.
Next time I'll order curry,
and at the end
I'll down the fortune cookie whole,
crunching passionately,
without looking.

Sauce and Redemption

We often believe
the theology and cooking
offered by seers who know
and persuade our belief
about God and cream sauce.
We may not understand
the fate of redemption
or the pleasure of sauce
but we do not care
when our belief
rests in a seer who does.

Flutter Bye

My mind embraces
  the thought of you
My body remembers
  each kiss and where
My heart alights
  upon the notion of loving you
  and
    trembles
Like the monarch upon
  warm pavement in autumn,
    as if to the rhythm
    of approaching traffic

Rosemary is Forever

We drank together and spoke of farewells
Knowing that tomorrow would be different
And apart.
We drank together and spoke of tomorrows
When our teacups would be empty and cold.
"Rosemary is forever," warned the old woman.
"Sip once and you cannot die apart," said she,
As we spoke of farewells and tomorrows.
Tomorrow has come. Tomorrow has gone.
Rosemary still lingers.
Our farewells have no meaning
Though our teacups are steaming
With chamomile prepared by different hands.
We have sipped of Rosemary
And lost our lives in a cup of tea.

Theodora Fair

15

Grandma's Meatloaf

L et the cold weather begin! Let the leaves fall, the northern winds blow. Minnesotans don't care about the arrival of winter because we know when it gets colder, we can start eating real food. High in carbohydrates, it fuels the body for frigid below-zero temperatures and sub-arctic wind chills. This food shines like a candle in the window, calling us home.

In October, when the leaves are almost off the trees, I begin craving the comfort food of my childhood. Comfort food is simple food, cooked from recipes that have been handed down from one generation of women to the next. Food cooked from scratch, by women who offered nourishment through times when money was scarce. Their recipes could feed a large family, with enough leftovers to use for lunch the next day.

My maternal grandmother made the most wonderful meatloaf. I can still see her in her kitchen, an apron over her house dress, using dishes and kitchen utensils that I now find in antique stores. Grandma would take one pound of hamburger, add a couple of eggs, some oatmeal, a little onion, and some milk, and make a high, rounded loaf. Served with ketchup, a baked potato, a vegetable; there was bread and butter, too. As a child, I liked the brown crusty part of the meat that cracked on the top after it was baked. Any leftovers were made into tomorrow's lunch, sandwiched between two slices of bread.

One of my best loved possessions today is the *Household Searchlight Recipe Book* inherited from my grandmother. I like to read the recipes, written in her own hand, on the yellowing bits of paper that are tucked in between the pages. I can see what foods she liked to cook, and guess, by the conditions of the pages, which recipes were her favorites.

When I was first married, I learned how to make my great-grandmother's Swedish rye bread. Aunt Laverne, my father's sister, gave me the recipe. As an adult, Laverne had to reconstruct it, based on her memory of watching her grandma in the kitchen because Maria never used recipes.

Making Swedish rye bread has become one of my Christmas traditions. Some years I may not bake many cookies, but I always make at least one batch of bread.

When I am scalding the milk, kneading the dough, smelling the pungent spiciness of the molasses, I am lulled into a slower rhythm. I cannot hurry through the process. Letting the dough rise twice, shaping the loaves to rise again, takes the better part of a day.

When I make the bread, I think about Maria, the immigrant from Sweden, who left her family and friends to start over in a new land. Homesteading on a farm in Rush City, Minnesota, she raised seven children. Stories of her are few, but I do know that she was a good cook. She offered a standing invitation every Sunday, when all of the family would come for chicken dinner. I imagine the Petersons, talking and laughing, sitting around a big table, buttering Maria's Swedish rye bread.

Two years ago, my beloved Aunt Laverne died of a sudden heart attack. Now, I am not only thankful that she passed the bread recipe along to me, but I also cherish the card that she has written on, even though it is stained, and curled on the edges.

All too often, the stories of our ancestors are lost. The stories that are missing the most, sadly, are the stories of the women. Busy working, struggling to survive, they did not always have time to record their thoughts and feelings. We may have birth dates written in Bibles, or death dates etched on tombstones, but often their personal stories have been forgotten. We have lost the essence of their personalities.

We are left to guess, looking through recipes, stroking the fragile pieces of paper, the artifacts of the women who lived before us. As I use their recipes, I imagine their presence around me. My grandmother, Christine, my great-grandmother, Maria, my aunt Laverne. I use the recipes from my mother, Joann, and my husband's mother, Eunice, and from friends, some of whom I have lost touch with over the years. I feel connected to the good women in my family, the generations before, and the generations to come.

I wonder if someday, Kendra, my baby granddaughter will stand in her kitchen, using one of my recipes? Will she stand, stirring, contemplating the phases of her life, as I have in mine?

A couple of years ago, after a particularly sad time in my life, I came home, discovering the real meaning of comfort food. My husband, Jeff, had cooked dinner. He had not cooked just any dinner, he had cooked my grandma's meatloaf. Now, my husband likes my grandma's meatloaf well enough, but it is not his favorite meal. It's definitely not a meal he would choose to make, but he made it for me because he knew it was my comfort food.

As I ate the supper, with tears dripping into my catsup, I knew that this was the sweetest thing he had ever done for me. Flowers, cards, dinners in restaurants, would never compare with this simple gesture: he made Grandma's meatloaf just for me and I was comforted with the presence of my grandma.

Comfort food does not have be fancy cuisine from a four-star restaurant. Comfort food is simple food, probably our favorite food, because it evokes memories of the women we have loved. Day after day, standing in their kitchens, they cooked for their families, using basic ingredients. We will never be able to truly comprehend the sacrifices they made, or the hardships they endured, but when we use their recipes we can honor their spirits. Cooking is so much more than food preparation. Food cooked with love is nourishment for the soul.

And so, like William Cowper I say:

"O Winter, ruler of the inverted year!
I love thee, all unlovely as thou seem'st,
And dreaded as thou art...
I crown thee king of intimate delights,
Fireside enjoyments, home-born happiness."

And in my mind I think: brown rice and chicken, beef stew, vanilla pudding, gingerbread with warm lemon sauce, cold weather cookies, Swedish meatballs, apple squares, boiled dinner, chicken and dumplings, split pea soup with crusty cornbread, rice pudding, mashed potatoes, meatloaf,Swedish rye bread. Comfort food, comfort food, comfort food.

mOJAKKA

bLOCK PRINT

Keith Hendrickson

Sandra VanCampen

Hunger for Hope

She lay down to die. There didn't seem to be any options left. The food had been gone for several days. The fierce January cold and never-ending snow prevented walking to the neighbors even if they had been closer. She was getting too weak even to make the trip to the little grove of cottonwoods behind the tiny cabin to get fuel for the fire.

In the twilight from the stove, she made out the shadowy images in the room. Emma's eyes rested on the two still forms under the blanket in the corner, her sons. John, the baby, was small to begin with. He needed more nourishment than her dwindling supply of breast milk and the thin cornmeal mush she'd coaxed him to take. He died first. The ground was frozen so she couldn't bury him, and she wouldn't lay him outside where animals might take him. Tommy, named for his father, was older and stronger. She thought he would be all right, until he started to cough and run a fever. He died yesterday.

Emma turned away from the dim light and felt the tears coming again. Tears of anguish, frustration, and fear. She drew Dottie, her oldest, closer to her, for warmth and comfort. She could feel the little girl's bones easily through the flannel of her nightdress. Dottie had stopped asking for anything to eat.

"Please God," she prayed, "take Dottie next. Don't make her wake up next to a corpse. She'd be so frightened." She'd stopped praying for Thomas to return or for someone to rescue them. Hope was gone on those counts.

As Thomas came to mind, she felt the rage build again. How could he have done this to them? She remembered when they'd first started courting. Thomas had dreams. He wasn't always going to be a farm hand. They saved their money carefully so they could move west and get their own spread. Not dairy cattle though. No, he would have a ranch in the Dakotas. He wasn't going to spend his life mucking out barns being chained to a milking schedule. A real man could be his own boss and set his own rules. Emma had admired his resolve and independent spirit. She hadn't seen signs of trouble back then.

He'd been very disappointed when Dottie was born. He'd wanted a son. Things seemed different between them after that. He was harsh with her and their daughter. Emma gave birth to Tommy the summer after they moved west, and Thomas

20

was thrilled. An heir for his ranch.

Ranch life was a big adjustment for Emma, being so far removed from town and even from neighbors. She was used to farms being smaller and closer together. Their nearest neighbors, the Martins, were five miles away. In the summer, they would ride over in the wagon occasionally, but once winter set in she didn't see anyone but Thomas and the children for months. When Thomas was gone, it was as if the world had evaporated leaving only her and their babies. Sometimes she thought she would go mad with fear and loneliness.

When the problems came, they came in quantity. Cattle prices were low. What had helped Thomas get started was what hurt him later when he started trying to sell the cattle. One dry year followed another, and the stream became a trickle. The hot dry summer burned up the grass the cattle fed on, as well as her garden. A few cattle died. Thomas erected a windmill to pump water for the cattle, but a storm demolished it. Illness broke out among the cattle and several more died. Thomas grew quiet and moody.

John was born last summer. He came early and was small but healthy. Thomas came out of his brooding and declared her again to be a gem of a wife, and then left for town to celebrate. He hadn't come back for a week. When he did return, he had supplies. He'd been offered some work he explained. And they needed the money. But he smelled of liquor and had a bottle of whiskey with him. The pattern continued through the summer and fall. Sometimes he was only gone overnight. No work. No money. No supplies. Other times he was gone several days. He always came back with liquor. And he was always mean when he drank. All of them, except the baby, had felt his hand across their face and all had been bruised by a harsh shove into a wall or table.

In the fall, he took several cattle to town to sell. He took the family along and Emma was able to pick out material to sew clothing for them all. They put in a supply of flour, cornmeal, oats, sugar, salt, and other staples. Not as much as she would have liked, but Thomas thought it would be enough. It was a happy time, but Emma cringed when she saw Thomas lift a case of whiskey bottles into the wagon. He caught her look, and said sharply, "Good for coughs and such."

As winter set in, Emma thought Thomas would not be going to town as often. While he had whiskey, he didn't. But when the supply was gone, so was Thomas.

As the days passed, Emma became terrified of the isolation. She had no way to get help if she needed it. He had the only horse, and the children could not walk the long distance to the nearest neighbor. The last time he returned, she told him how frightened she'd been, how dangerous it was for her and the children to have no way to get help, and how much they needed him. He didn't respond. He sat down in the rocker and opened a bottle, all the time staring at her with eyes of ice. Emma's heart turned to stone at that moment. She knew she could never love him again.

A few days later, Thomas started packing his saddlebag. Emma begged him to stay or at least to hitch up the wagon and take them all to town. "You can do whatever you want then," she cried, "I'll leave you alone. I'll find some work. You can't leave us here."

At first, Thomas was reassuring. "I know I've left you alone too much," he said. "I won't be gone long. I need to see if there's any work for me. Our supplies aren't going to last the winter."

"Take us with you," Emma screamed. "You can"t leave us here alone again. We could die."

Thomas turned cold again. "Don't you ever raise your voice to me again," he shouted, and the blows started coming. When Emma came to, the children were crying, the light was fading, and the fire was low. Thomas was gone. She'd lost track of how long ago that was.

The memories faded as she drifted off to sleep. "Please, God," she prayed desperately, "Let us be among your angels."

The sound of dripping water woke her. Confused, she instinctively reached for Dottie. Still alive. Then Emma realized the sound came from outside. Looking out the window, she saw rivulets of water running off the roof. She heard the whistle of a strong wind, and it came to her. Chinook! A winter thaw. She opened the door and felt the air. Hope enveloped her like an embrace. She felt strength surge through her body as she considered the possibilities. Yes. It was warm enough to try.

"Dottie," she cried. "Wake up. God sent us a miracle. We're going to walk to the Martins for help."

Dottie looked confused, but was obviously reassured by her mother's face. "Will there be food there?" Dottie asked hopefully.

"Yes, sweetheart," Emma answered. "Hurry and get dressed. I don't know how long this weather will hold."

Emma gathered their coats, boots and hats. She picked up the two blankets on the bed, rolled them into a bundle, and tied them so she could carry them on her back. She wasn't sure how long it would take to reach their neighbors with the snow to contend with and she didn't want to be unprepared if the temperature started to drop again.

She started leave, but paused when she thought of her sons. She turned to the still forms in the corner. "I'm so sorry, babies," she murmured softly. "I'm sorry I couldn't save you." Sorrow threatened to overwhelm her, but she forced herself to turn away. She took a deep breath and said a prayer. Resolutely, she walked out the door.

They started down the long drive to the road. "I'm scared, Mama," Dottie said softly.

She squeezed her daughter's small hand in hers. The sun felt warm against her face. Emma looked down at the frightened child and smiled. "God didn't save us to let us die now, Dottie," resolve filling her voice. "And God doesn't expect His miracles to fail."

The two pushed their way through the snow. Emma looked back for a moment at the cabin. It had started out a sanctuary, filled with hope. Now it was a tomb. Remembering the cold whisper of death she'd sensed the night before, she felt a new force liberated from deep within. "I'll never give up again." she said. "Never."

Author's Note: This is a fictional story inspired by experiences of my maternal grandmother. She died almost fifty years ago, and she is the only one who would have known the facts. All I know is that she must have been a very strong woman to have survived the desperate conditions and the death of her two young sons. She divorced her husband (unheard of in those days) and remarried. My mother was the first child of that union. I've heard that in her new life, she set a generous table, and that the men in the threshing crews were especially fond of this pie (on page 24).

Sandra VanCampen

Apple Cream Pie

4 to 6 baking apples
1 unbaked pie crust
1 cup sugar
2 tablespoons flour
1 cup rich cream
Dash salt
Dash or two nutmeg
1 teaspoon cinnamon

Line unbaked crust with peeled, sliced apples. Mix flour, sugar and seasonings. Add cream and mix. Pour over apples. Bake for 50-60 minutes at 375 degrees.

Memory of Tomorrow

Casey Mitchell

Goals running through my mind
Uniquely my own
Original as a snowflake

Predetermined by myself
My future stands bold
Vivid as a rainbow

Sometimes hiding behind a cloud
My hopes and dreams
Fade away like a sunset

My direction and aspirations stay in my heart
Success and happiness
Rely on memories made with tomorrows.

24

Carson Gardner   Jayson Knutson

Chocolate Chip

Truth is a chocolate chip cookie—
more than its ingredients,
less than its recipe,
wondrous in the mouth,
useless in the jar;
prized for its flavor
not for its oven.

chocolate

So delicate,
So rich,
So...So,
very addictive
is chocolate,
but "O" So
good,
you have to have,
just a little more.

¢HOCOLATE ¢HIP ¢OOKIES
ᵇLOCK PRINT

Lacey Roiko

Flour Sack Underwear

Money was scarce in the 30's for a family of 12 kids. My mother made our clothing out of flour sacks and chicken feed sacks.

When I was a maiden fair,
Mama made our underwear.
With twelve tots, and Pa's poor pay,
How could she buy us lingerie?
Monograms and fancy stitches,
Were on our flour sack britches.
Robin Hood or Pillsbury Best,
Five Roses seal upon our chest.
Little pants were best of all,
With a scene I still recall.
Robin Hood, where gleaming wheat
Ran right across the little seat.
Tougher than a grizzly bear
Was our flour sack underwear.
Plain or fancy, three feet wide
Stronger than a hippo's hide.
Through the years, each Jill and Jack
Wore this garment made of sack.
Waste not want not, you soon learned,
A penny saved is a penny earned.
Bed spread, curtains, tea towels too,
And table cloths used thru and thru.
Best of all, beyond compare,
Was our flour sack underwear.

Home Made Soap*

*Lye is extremely caustic. Follow manufacturer's directions for safety precautions.

In an earthen jar put 1 can Luis lye and 2 quarts of cold water. Let this cool, as lye heats up water. Let it set over night.

Stir often with wooden paddle at first. When it's cool, add 2 quarts of shortening lard or 2 quarts plus 2 cups of vegetable shortening.

Add 1/2 cup baking soda dissolved in 1 cup ammonia. Stir well and pour into a paper box lined with plastic or wax paper. Soap will be thick, so cut into bars.

Let it rest 3 days before using.

David Sanders

The Cook in the Kitchen, Cooking a Chicken
(an excerpt from Return to Kwetu, a novel-in-progress)

Mark awoke his first morning in Africa to find himself in a darkened room and a small bed. At first, the room appeared to the drowsy boy to be filled with a light mist. But a sweep of his arm revealed a fine, white netting that hung from the ceiling and draped down around the bed on all sides. Along the side of his arm where it had rested against the netting, a line of mosquito bites now begged to be scratched.

He slid under the netting and stood in the soft light in his underwear, his bare feet cool on the cement floor. He found his glasses on the corner of a small desk and placed them carefully on his face, their black frames a stark contrast to his pale skin and short-cropped, red hair. The room's furnishings, he could now see, were simple: desk, chair, dresser, rough weaving on the wall, and a child's bed hidden beneath a cloud of mosquito netting. His travel clothes were draped over the chair, and he quickly slipped back into their familiar scent and feel. He lifted the window blind and late morning sun flooded in. When he opened his door, more brilliant light filled the room. He walked down the hall and into the small living room, feeling like an intruder in this silent, foreign house. Idly scratching his arm, he tried to make sense of his new surroundings—the spare wood furniture, the concrete floor covered with rough, woven rugs, and the lush, green foliage outside the windows.

A noise drew him to the kitchen. From the archway, he watched a tall man in tan pants and white short-sleeve shirt knead dough on a wooden table. The man looked up from his work and grinned broadly at Mark, his sweat-stained face a deep, glistening black. He spoke in a low, rumbling voice that swept Mark along its current.

"*Jambo, bwana* Morgan! You slept well—like a lion cub! I am glad."

The man wiped his finger energetically on a white towel wrapped around his waist, and extended an enormous hand toward the boy. The back of his hand was like charcoal, dark black and cracked with scars an crevices. The palm was a light brown, coarse and deeply creased, with flecks of dough still clinging between his fingers.

"Welcome to Kwetu! I am Chege. Chege Ndegwa, your cook."

Mark took the hand tentatively and shook it. The man laughed a deep, growling laugh.

"Ahh, good! What a strong, little man you are! You did not know you would have your own cook, eh? I am a very good cook, I assure you. But you will soon know that for yourself, eh? Can you say this? 'The cook is in the kitchen, cooking a chicken!' Yes? No so easy for Kikuyu cook to say in English. A Kikuyu cook, eh! Another tongue twisting! But maybe not too difficult for a smart boy from the American States?"

Mark was lost, awash in this rush of words.

"Your father is gone to work this morning. His first day here, eh? A hard worker! But only for a short while is he gone. He is holding a meeting with your neighbor, Mr. Alongo. Very good, very important man, Mr. Alongo. Important to Kwetu. Important to Kenya and independence. A mighty spear. You will learn. And your father, too. A very brave, very good man to come to Kenya to teach the teachers. Aha! Another good one! 'The teacher is teaching the teachers to teach!' You must practice that one, too! Your father said I am to tell you that he will be home for lunch. And that is what I am now preparing. *Kuku na mkate* , eh? A fresh chicken stew with fresh baked bread. But first! Here are biscuits for your breakfast. And a ripe banana from your very own banana tree. And juice from your very own oranges, right outside. Did you know you have such a garden? Eh, I bet you want to go and explore your new home, yes? Your new world! So eat your food! Then go."

Mark stood mutely at the table and ate his breakfast slowly while he watched Chege pound the dough, turn it into a large wooden bowl, cover it with a cloth, and with a graceful stretch, set the bowl up high atop an old, rusting refrigerator. With a flourish, the cook leaned down, pulled an onion from a basket on the concrete floor, and placed it on a plank of wood on the table top. Several quick, rolling chops of a large knife reduced the onion to pieces, which Chege threw into a pan on the stove to dance in hot oil. Another sweeping bow to the floor retrieved a second onion, and with two flick of his wrist, Chege divided it into quarters, which he dropped into a large pot of boiling water. Like a conjurer, the tall man rubbed his hands together, reached high up into the corner of the small kitchen, and pulled something down from a hook in the ceiling. It took Mark several seconds to recognize the object as a skinny, roughly plucked, headless chicken, which Chege now held by the neck. He place the grayish body on the wood plank, and with a few graceful movements had the bird skinned, disemboweled, cracked and cut into pieces. A few more passes with the knife, and the meat was magically boned and cut into chunks. The chicken's stomach was tossed in the sink for cleaning. The giblets, skin and bones all went into the boiling water. The cut meat joined the sizzling onions. With another slight of hand, Chege produced a fistful of carrots from seemingly nowhere, and quickly dispatched them into thick slices that followed the meat into the pan.

By now, Mark had finished his breakfast. He wiped his mouth on his arm and spoke softly, afraid to break the spell the cook had cast.

"May I go outside now?"

Chege turned, a potato having somehow appeared in his hand, and smiled kindly down on the boy.

"Ah, little *bwana* , you are a very polite, young man. Of course! Go, explore. I will call for you when your father returns."

Mark placed his dishes in the sink and stepped tentatively toward the open doorway. He was stopped by the view that greeted him. It *was* a new world waiting out there. Beyond the concrete slab of the back porch, an expanse of tall grass swept up a steep hillside to his right. He took another step into the doorway itself, and stopped again. Up the hill, along the right side of the yard, a small garden was cut into the steep slope of the mountain. Two orange trees provided shade for stands of bananas, pineapple, sugar cane and rows of various vegetables. He glanced to his left. There, a long, tall hedge of tended bushes and stalks of bamboo separated his yard from that of his neighbors, the Alongos.

Straight ahead, though, loomed the most dramatic feature of his backyard— the towering wall of the jungle itself. Rising abruptly from the edge of the grass, the imposing veil of trees and vines was startling in its sudden, alien wildness. Intimidating. Enticing.

Chege stood behind him. "Yes, it is very beautiful, eh? A beautiful, proud country. So, go! Go, explore!"

Mark stepped into the brilliant Kenyan sun. Chege called out after him.

"And young *bwana* !" Mark turned, but could only see the ghost of Chege's outline against the kitchen's shadow. "Watch out for the lions and the leopards. I don't want you eaten before your father comes home!"

Chege rumbled with laughter and returned to his chopping, disappearing into the dark shade of the kitchen.

Kedjenou

This dish hails from the Ivory Coast of Africa, where it is cooked in a clay pot, or canari, which is sealed with a banana leaf. Use a flameproof, heavy-lidded enameled or cast-iron casserole. The kedjenou can be served with white rice instead of the traditional attieke, a fermented starch.

Makes 4 servings

2 1/2 to 3 pound chicken, cut into eight pieces
2 medium onions
Sliced carrots, (optional)
2 tablespoons minced ginger
1 clove of garlic, minced
1 bay leaf
Salt and freshly ground pepper

Place the chicken, onions, carrots, ginger, garlic and bay leaf in the casserole and season with salt and pepper. Cover tightly and cook over moderately low heat for about 40 minutes, shaking the casserole every 5 minutes to prevent sticking. Do not uncover the casserole during cooking. Discard the bay leaf before serving.

Cosmic Soup

from the green hills of Earth to the cold frozen plains of Titan
not a long step, in one's imagination.
bright blade of starlight against dark shield of blackened space.
what hides Out There?
and the armor of a planet-fragile melding of oxygen and swirling ozone
even frailer the creatures who crawl under this blazing life-giver that rules our skies
struck down so carelessly—yet we care.
look outward, oh curious one
what strange creatures roam the airless deserts of the dark side of the moon,
'eyes' turned away from the hot emissions of the star that moves
coupled in ancient embrace with her almost twin
warped mirror of the larger mother system
Jupiter turns and Io burns, twisting space around it
drawing wayward travelers of the void into his deadly embrace.
do gaseous electric entities graze in the fast-spinning hydrogen clouds of this great giant?
mostly icy chondrites out here
and the red ones—is there any such thing as space lichen?
still further out—the frozen power plants of Neptune and Uranus.
why didn't they name it George instead?
and the last one—not even a planet some think.
what lurks there, still undiscovered, on the solar system's front door.
Kyper's belt turns out there, flinging inward the occasional outcast of space.
leftovers of the birth of star-system.
will we mine there someday? Live there and love there?
ice such as no inner planet will ever see, unless catastrophe strikes too soon...
just another blot on Mother Nature's ink pad.
until she tries again.

WILD ⁰NIONS
HAND ᶜOLORED ᵇLOCK PRINT

Steve Norlin

Shannon Geisen

For Love, Onions

An old farmer's wife chops onions for spicy potato soup,
a favorite recipe, worn thin at the edges
by sticky fingers and liquid spots.
It's one that her husband had loved.

Probably been forty years since she last made it.

And as she unravels the flaky, outer skin of the onion,
the familiar sting returns.
Her blue eyes are quick to water.

She smiles a little, recalling her husband's love
for the hottest ingredients—jalapeño, green chili peppers, picante sauce.

Well past suppertime, he would return from the barn,
smelling of tractor oil and stomping his work boots.
Wearing tan overalls stained with grease spots.

He would tease her, seeing the tears leaking from her eyes.
Then, turning soft, he'd say,
I tell cows about you.

Her wrist shakes. It's getting difficult to hold the cutting knife.
I'm getting old, says the farmer's wife,
though no one can hear.
She blinks back more tears.

Isn't it funny, she thinks, how love brings
the same ache as making spicy potato soup.
How the quiet, unspoken cuts a throat to shreds.
Makes eyes bleed like onions do.

Boppa's Beer Battered Fish

We highly recommend this dish be served with the Cosmic Soup found on page 31.

1 cup flour
1 egg
Salt to taste
Pepper to taste
Approximately 1/2 can of beer
Fresh fish

Use enough beer to make the mix the consistency of pancake batter.

Fill a heavy frying pan with 2 inches of oil and heat until very hot. Dip your freshly caught Minnesota fish into the batter and fry until golden brown.

This batter can also be used to deep fry vegetable, mushrooms and seafood.

Walk

Bright sun
shines through my vision.
I see clouds,
translucent and puffy-cotton.
I walk through
potato-chip leaves,
rusty brown, snapping
beneath my stretching legs and
my heavy toes.
Please shine until I die.
The sun is making the leaves
become red (like a cherry lollipop)
and yellow (like a lemon one)
for a blink only.
When I open my eyes once more
I notice the empty world above me;
it's filled with nothing, yet
looks like pictures of people.

One day, the world got dark at
6 p.m. and the trees had no more leaves.
I shivered when I saw the cottony clouds
and drew a scarf over the neck
that the wind drew its hands around,
suddenly.

I wonder at life, and ask if I should
control it or not, as if
I had the choice or the time
for such luxurious options
on this day when the sun shines brightly
through my vision,
making every leaf the color of fruit.

Harvesting the Bounty

The crops are bearing fruit. The trees are turning golden. My brother and Dad are filling the barn with hay for winter feed. Northern Minnesota's short growing season makes summer a busy time for anyone living on a farm. This past summer's cool temperatures put all crops late in their maturing. Peas in the garden came into full bloom after the middle of August and were still filling pods when I pulled the vines last week.

Each year has its own struggle to face. The years of repeated drought in these Northwoods are too recent. Even as I look out on mist-drenched leaves this September morn, drought still haunts my memory. No matter what the weather gives, the summer's produce must be packed away to feed and nurture through the coming winter.

The stacks in the hay yard lengthen as loads of large round bales are hauled in. I straighten my back from another picking of beans to watch the tractors pull into the yard. The heavy wagon creaks from side to side through every dip in the farmyard. I smile, wave, and bend back to my task.

Later, as the chugging of the tractors fades back toward the field, I hear the whup, whup of beating wings and look up to see a large red-tailed hawk flying very low over the garden in his circling. I think, "Where are my chickens?" Then I remember—I have a net over the pen ever since a hawk helped himself to one of my pullets earlier this year. He was harvesting in his way, too.

Across the road from the end of the drive, a dead calf lies in the pasture. The eagles and turkey buzzards have moved in for a feeding. Seven of them perched overhead on sturdy branches of standing dead trees. On a farm nothing goes to waste. When they are done with the carcass, the mice and chipmunks will come to gnaw for calcium on the exposed bones.

The squirrels mass harvest the acorns as they cut another and another from the branch in the oaks near the chicken pen. Acorns rain upon my head. Chattering squirrels descend the trunks to carry fallen fruit to private storage with a logic only they understand.

Just last week, bees busily harvested nectar from purple thistle blooms that stretched up to my bedroom window in the sunshine.

Years ago, as I floated down the river in a canoe, I watched as a muskrat on the bank mowed a row of grass with his teeth. He laid the bunch in a neat pile and

35

repeated with four more rows. Stuffing all the bunches in his mouth, he came down to the water's edge dragging the long ends behind. The muskrat swam along the shore and disappeared into a hole in the bank. He was harvesting hay for his family's winter food supply.

I harvest from nature, too. Roadside wild flower bouquets have been tied to hang upside down inside paper bags to retain their color. They will cheer a future drab February day with their beauty.

That scoundrel Jack Frost had been active in the community, teasing the young-maiden maples till they blush. I watch an old maple just outside my kitchen window. When the leaves are mottled red and green I go pick a few for the house. I'm watching for some mature, dark brown, wild tobacco to add to the bouquet. Usually I reach into the pond for some cattails, but this year the water is too high.

The woods abound with harvest, too. We are blessed with many wild fruits on our farm: plums, strawberries, June berries, raspberries, blackberries and chokecherries. I always considered any wild fruit a gift from God that should not be squandered. So, when the wild plums are read I go lay an old sheet around the trunk of the tree. I give the branch over the sheet a firm shake. Then I pick up the plums that landed on the ground and toss them onto the sheet also. After repeating the pattern for all branches, I gather the corners of the sheet up into my hand and sling the plum-filled bundle over my shoulder like a backpack for the trudge back home.

Last year, being in a hurry, I discovered the easiest plum jam recipe. I cooked the plums in very little water just until the skins cracked. Then I cooled the batch so I could remove the seeds. I put small batches into the blender to chop coarsely. Then I cooked it all up for jam. The skins gave the jam a special rich red color, but the best part was the tart taste.

Back in the garden, the raspberries gave their last ripe fruit a month ago, but the rest of the garden is bearing now. Tomatoes slowly turning red as they ripen in the late summer sun.

After a while I develop a routine. I pick fresh peas or beans in the afternoon when the garden is dry. Then into the evening hours I am shelling or snapping the harvest. In the cool of the morning, my kitchen steams at the seams while the pressure cooker whistles its merry tune of "This is the way we preserve our food, so early in the morning." Later, as the jars cool down, each 'ping' of a jar lid is music to my ears.

This year, my uncle gave me yellow and green bean seeds. He saves seed each year from his growing crop. I ended up with a few green bean plants in the yellow row and vice versa. So, I didn't pick the beans in the wrong row and let them get large for my seed next year. I have them laid out in a sunny exposure to dry now. Later, I will crush the outer shell and save just the seed.

I'm letting the green beans on the plants grow larger for Leather Britches. I snip the ends and dry the whole bean thoroughly in a warm dry place in the house. After they are dried these beans left in the shell can be placed in a paper bag and hung from a rafter. To prepare them for eating, I soak them overnight in the shell, just like regular dry beans, before cooking with smoked ham hocks for a hearty soup.

My root crops were sporadic in this year's cool soil. Some did poorly, a half a grocery bag of potatoes from four rows; some did well, turnips the size of melons. But my carrots really produced, easily a bushel per row.

My carrots have not kept well the last couple years. My friend suggested layering them in sand. "In dry sand," my sister added. So, this year, I will dry some sand in my oven and layer the carrots in a large plastic bucket and see how long they last. I will still store them in my sister's cool basement.

While digging, picking and pulling the last of the crop, I toss all the small vegetables, those tiny throwaways, into one pile. Last night Dad and I enjoyed that pile of onions, carrots, potatoes, rutabagas, turnips, cabbage, beans, green pepper and peas with venison stew from last November.

The venison wasn't exactly from the garden, but my niece did have her stew all from the garden years ago when they snared rabbits that were eating the veggies. My sister harvests even the slugs from her garden. Not for eating, she says, they are better than worms for fishing.

My car has smelled like a vegetable bin these past weeks as I tote produce from the garden up on the farm a quarter mile away to prepare for canning here or storage in my sister's dirt vegetable bin ten miles away. Sometimes the peas, beans and peppers just travel everywhere with me until I can get them preserved.

This time of year on a farm is very soul satisfying as we store away our treasures. It is a busy time, but deeply satisfying.

^bREAKFAST ^mUFFINS

^bLOCK PRINT

Lynn Keranen

Lisa McCallum

Ritual

I made myself coffee
last weekend
while cool air of September
floated in my kitchen window.
Sun dried water drips
on the counter
before I could rub
my finger through them.
When it was ready, I poured
half of the miniature carafe
into my mug.

How unexpectedly brown it was! I thought,
not having measured the grains.
I gathered sugar onto a big spoon
from my clean, white sugar bowl. I added
cold milk that whirled quickly, helped by
the breeze perhaps, into the brown,
making the sweet broth tan.
My cupboards smell of
these exotic beans; ripe, chocolaty.
Remember the ancient and quaint cafes of Linz?

On weekends, I will
make myself coffee.
I will proceed with
this ritual and recall
the fresh, ivory cream
in the tiny, steel cup
that sits alongside frothy
espresso in loud, smoky cafes.
I will smile at this memory, for I believe
that the deep brown coffee made
from South American beans
and mixed with clean sugar
and cold skim milk
from my refrigerator
tastes miraculously better.

Laine Cunningham

A Way to a Man's Heart

She prepares his pot roast
Potatoes and gravy
Congealed lumps of reheated devotion
She packs it snugly in his bag
Her oblation to keep him full and warm

He eats of it
Cleans his plate
And stops in my bed on his way home

Harold Huber

Change of Venue

I lifted from a daydream,
A poem on my heart.
Its warmth, at my sternum,
Spirit-scented, shimmering.

I stood motionless, silent.
No wakeful act to jostle
The newborn, still-warm words,
Nor their whispered music.

I plucked the poem from my heart,
Squeezed warmth through a pen,
Filtered lines through a keyboard,
Changed locale - heart to head.

Now on paper, there it shines,
Spiffed and polished,
Groomed and purified,
Cleansed of heartbeats...chilly...dead.

Corn Soup

I helped to braid the corn in the fall
and it hung heavy against the wall
in the unheated bedroom.
When our relatives came,
we dragged the long braids
into the kitchen and, sitting on the floor,
we twisted the corn off with our strong hands.
Then we pushed the stubborn kernels free
with our mighty thumbs.
Soon our hands were tired
and our thumbs were sore.
But we didn't stop until we finished.
I filled a large green bowl three times.
I remember the beauty of red and blue
and golden seeds filling the bowl,
offering themselves joyfully
for our well-being.
Together we filled an enamel pail
with dried corn.
Then Mama made it into hominy
and dried it again in muslin hammocks
which hung from the ceiling in the unheated room.
When our relatives came again,
they brought clean socks.
Mama filled them with hominy
and tied them shut.
Our relatives left, rich with corn.
Sometimes when my thumbs ache
with arthritis, I remember
how we helped Mama make hominy.
I remember the warm kitchen
full of happy people and
I remember her good
corn soup.

^tHE ^eNTERTAINER

^cONTE ^cRAYON

Steve Narlin

Calling Kuloskap

The low tremolo-wail broke the silence.

We looked over and saw a lone loon bobbing in the still-calm water.

"Roy, why do loons sometimes sing that really sad song at night?" Cynthia asked.

I smiled. Ever since Cynthia had left the hustle and bustle of California to start a life anew in Bemidji as my wife seven short years ago, questions like these would arise from time to time. Questions as to why things were the way they were in this under-populated, under-industrialized, seemingly bizarre land that was so far away from the overabundant strip malls and superhighways of her native Bay Area. And she knew I enjoyed answering them in my own way.

"Some say it's a call for companionship, attention, a cry of uncertainty, or . . ."

"Or what?"

"Or he's calling for Kuloskap to return," I replied.

"Excuse me," she exclaimed. She pulled my hand and we came to a stop. Being nine months pregnant, and on the verge of bringing our son into this mixed-up, yet grand world of ours, Cynthia's range of exercise had been limited to nightly walks up and about downtown, lingering jaunts at Lake Bemidji State Park, and our treasured treks down to the Lake Bemidji shoreline to watch the ducks. These walks also provided the perfect opportunities for husband and wife to discuss the day's events, the somewhat bewildering future, and whatever else readily came to mind.

This time we had wandered past the ever-vigilant statues of Paul and Babe well before twilight and watched the ducks and Canada geese cavort about until it slowly grew dark and a lone loon took the stage. Tonight his plaintive song would provide our last thread of discussion and I had casually tossed out yet another of my mythological analogies which Cynthia had no clue as to what to make of.

"Is this another one of your stories?" she softly asked.

I nodded, then wracked my brain for the full story. Finally, I recited the following: "Kuloskap was a godlike hero. . ." I winced a bit, knowing full well I had gone straight into lecture mode again.

"Where?"

I had definitely piqued her interest, my brusqueness easily forgiven. I eased up the tone. "In Maine and parts of East Coast Canada, this story comes from the Passamaquoddy."

"Oh." Cynthia pulled herself closer to me, and I put my arm around her as the wind picked up and the waves started to form.

"Kuloskap, otherwise known as Glaskoop, created all of the animals in the forest, and when he had completed this task, he went to mankind and showed him which animals and plants were good for food, and how to make the most of what he had to work with. He taught man how to hunt according to the laws of nature, and even taught him how to make and use the bow and arrow and the net. Man was happy, and there was great peace throughout the land. Unfortunately, man eventually became greedy and wasteful; he started to war amongst himself, and started abusing the gifts that Kuloskap had so generously given him

Kuloskap finally grew tired of man's rash and destructive behavior, and after much careful thought, decided to go off to other worlds and create anew.

So he gathered man and all of the animals in the forest by a great lake and put on a lavish feast for them. All that time, man and animals could all speak the same language, and as they feasted they sang song, told stories, danced, and had a joyous time. At the end of the great feast, Kuloskap climbed into his canoe, and set himself off adrift, singing the songs of glory and power he had used in creation. As he drifted further and further into the deep, dark recesses of the lake, his songs became fainter and fainter until he was heard and seen no more.

Those on shore watched with utter amazement, and when the last few notes of Kuloskap's song finally lingered away in the mist, man and the animals soon discovered they could no longer understand one another. They all left the feast site amongst the confusion, returning to their lives in the forest, and soon forgot the common language that had once bound them all together in peace and harmony. All, but Loon. Loon had been an old friend of Kuloskap's from the very beginning and was dismayed that Kuloskap was gone. In vain, Loon called and called in this universal common tongue for Kuloskap to return, but Kuloskap continued on into the darkness, and was never seen again."

"The expulsion from Garden of Eden and the Tower of Babel all in one," Cynthia firmly said. After a long pause came, "That is so sad."

I nodded, then finished the story. "You can still hear Loon at dawn or on a quiet evening calling for the mighty hero-creator to return. Sometimes Loon is joined by Wolf—others have cast Wolf in their stories in a role similar to that of Loon's—and you can sometimes hear loons and wolves howling together in seeming unison. Both wish to have great Kuloskap return and bring harmony back to all who live in the forest so all can live in peace without fear or want."

With that, there was a great quiet between us and we stood hand in hand as we watched the waves crash harder and harder against the shoreline. Finally, Cynthia squeezed my hand. We turned back toward the lights of downtown, and made our way home.

Loon had stopped calling for Kuloskap to return.

Wild Rice with Cashews

2 cups wild rice
1/3 cup butter or margarine
1/2 cup chopped cashews
2 cups fresh mushrooms, sliced
Fresh parsley, chopped

In a sieve, rinse wild rice under running water for two minutes and then drain. In a large saucepan, bring to boil enough lightly salted water to cover rice by three inches. Pour in rice. Cook for 30 minutes or until rice is tender. Drain rice and place in serving bowl. Saute mushrooms in a pan with butter, and pour over rice. Add cashews, and toss. Sprinkle with chopped parsley and serve. Makes 8 to 10 servings.

Venison Wild Rice Roll Ups

8 venison steaks, cut about 3/16-inches thick
Diced onion and celery (optional)
Salt and pepper
1 package brown gravy
Wild Rice with Cashews (see above recipe) to spread on the venison steaks.

Roll out the venison steaks and lightly season with salt and pepper. Spread on Wild Rice with Cashews to which you may add onion and celery, then roll up steaks tightly. Place roll ups, seam side down, in a lightly greased dish. Brown uncovered in a 350-degree oven for about 20 to 25 minutes. When the meat is browned, cover roll ups with brown gravy (which has been mixed up as directed on package). Return to oven and bake uncovered for approximately 30 minutes longer. Serve with bread and apple cider, and enjoy!

O Aglio! An Ode to Garlic

Slipping your silver iridescence off
in layers—petals, one
beneath another,
that promise pink
underlying abalone skin,
I come at last
instead to ivory—
early, early morning, shadowed green.
Your flesh is firm.
Your curves entice my slicing.

And I am not disappointed,
for by then
your breathed-in presence,
redolent in rich
memory, recalls my passion:
salami, pesto fettucine, aioli, chicken parmesan,
ratatouille, ravioli, roasted, melted cloves
to slip my
ardent tongue
upon.

Now my fingers, soaked in garlic,
stroke the air with fragrance.

Fumes.
Abide with me.

Vampires of pale nutrition suck

my life away in this bland, white
northern land, where boiled cabbage,
mashed potatoes, celery sticks
and plain pork roast demand
my gastronomic duty.

Is there no beauty
in these kitchens?
I do not eat to live.
I live to die in succulence piccante: aglio.

To ward off vampires, my amulet,
I vow
I would have you hung about my neck
to tell the world I love you.

I would breathe out
your memory
in every word I speak.

     Oh heavy breath.

I would attract
only your legions. Others can stay
palely,

     properly,

         apathetically
away.

Theodora Fair   Fern Feller

Minnesota Eucharist   ## French Bread

December thickens the blood,   I was walking across twenty-first
And stiffens the bone.   street
The river slows then stops.   devouring a baguette
The woods are stark and silent.   surprised at the tingle of salt
The harvest, what there was of it, left on my lips.
Is counted and stored.
                                    A man in his car
We stand in the frozen field   rubbernecking as I peeled back
Hands clasped,   the bag
Heads thrown back,   looked at me as if I were
Breath rising white to the leaden sky, holding...him.
Waiting in rapt expectation,
To taste the sweetness   I thought:
Of the first flake on the tongue,   I'm so hungry
To know the final forgiveness   why wait until home?
Of snow.
                                    He thought:
                                    She's so hungry
                                    She's so hungry.

                                    The flaky bread
                                    pink-stained with lipstick
                                    left crumbs of satisfaction
                                    adorning my mouth.

                                    By the time
                                    the light turned green
                                    half of it was gone
                                    inside me.

                                    Horns were blaring

                                    The driver
                                    still not ready to go
                                    was tantalized
                                    by the metaphor.

48

Caramelized Onion Tart

1 package Pepperidge Farm Puff
  Pastry Shells
3 to 4 medium onions, sliced
2 cloves of fresh garlic, finely
  chopped. Let it sweat for at least
  10 minutes to enhance flavor.
3 tablespoons olive oil or butter
2 tablespoons brown sugar
Herbes de Provence (optional)

Bake pastry shells according to directions. Set aside, and cover with a clean cloth to keep warm. Heat the olive oil or butter in a non-stick skillet. Add the garlic and onions and cook over low to medium-low heat until the onions are soft and golden. This may take 20 to 30 minutes. Do attend to the filling mixture, stirring constantly and gently as you do not want to overcook and burn the holy onions.
When the onions have reach a golden color, sprinkle the brown sugar over all, and stir gently. Remove the skillet from the stove. Spoon the filling into the pastry shells. Top with herbes de Provence, if you wish. Serve immediately. Serves 4 to 6 people as an appetizer.

Author's Note: *Though I have taken a class from a French chef at Cook's on Grand Avenue in St. Paul to learn the art of tarte l'oignon, and traveled to France and eaten this special dish, I admit to laziness; hence, this is an Americanized version of onion tart.*

Flavor of the Heart

Picked for your size, bulbous shape
and satiny purple skin, you boss the cart,
get carried home in separate bag
to avoid bruising by soup cans.

I set you in sterling. Keep knives away
For days you monopolize
the kitchen counter
safe in my custody.

Your thin skin makes me cry. I know
full well the flavor of your heart—chamber
of sweet tears, the violet ribbons within
How lovely you'd be on mixed green.

Knowing our tearful theatrics I vow not
to cut you, stinking rose, nor intrude
upon your fragrant beauty,
but offer you up whole:
A planet spinning. A blossom sculpted
in gold. Centerpiece for table or mantle.
Bauble for Christmas tree. A spell, a charm,
a chaser of evil. Talisman for Giant, perhaps
the Cardinal's heavenly hat.

Then again,
I could peel your pretty belly,
slice you, dice and chop,
cook away tomorrow
savor your sugary heart
in a caramelized onion tart.

49

^sTEAMING JAVA
^bLOCK PRINT

Seth Baso

The Best Coffee

The best coffee I ever had
still warms my heart,
makes me laugh and wonder.
She sold it straight black,
poured in simple beauty,
sweetened with an honest smile,
stirred to the soul
by her cinnamon touch
on my sleeve,
served with a chocolate secret—
of no consequence—
that made me taste
younger days
when I, too,
might have vied
for her mocha passion.
This old fool,
old that day, already,
still knows magic in my cup
well enough
to sparkle with the glow
of unselfconscious dreaming.
The best coffee I ever had
steams in memory
of that day
a nameless java goddess
made it cappuccino,
for a stranger,
with the milk of romance.

The Witches' Supermarket

At the Witches' Supermarket
All their milk is sour
And all their grapes.
The bakery has gingerboys and gingergirls
And Wonder Bread.
Variety meats are in demand:
Hearts and livers, eyes and brains.

They sell in season night- and sun-shade,
Poisonous mushrooms canned or dried,
Boxes of Witch's Helper,
All brands on sale
(The very thing to stretch a spell
When it doesn't matter
What you transform to,
Just so it's improved and new.)

The change they make at check-out registers
Will curdle you.

^SPILT MILK
^bLOCK PRINT

Jamie Juntti

Off Course

My adventures in the kitchen have been widely varied, reflecting the various stages of my life. As a kid, I first learned to make the basics at home—peanut butter sandwiches, spaghettios, canned soup. Cooking in my college dorm was challenging, using a popcorn popper that with proper coaxing and watchfulness could also be used to make macaroni and cheese, mashed potatoes, soup, pudding and other comfort foods.

During my vegetarian years I struggled to make tofu and textured vegetable protein appetizing, with varying degrees of success. My strange-ingredient period was characterized by an attraction to recipes with unlikely components, like cakes made with sauerkraut or tomato soup. In my gourmet phase, I made Baked Alaska, baklava, and lasagna, all from scratch.

Success is enjoyable at the time, but in the long run, disasters make better stories. So, I present to you a menu of some of my most interesting culinary disasters.

My first major cooking disaster was a dessert. Back when I had just learned to read, I thought I was old enough to start doing things in the kitchen by myself. I announced to my mother that I wanted to make peanut butter cookies, and I was going to make them by myself. She helped me get out the ingredients and find the recipe in the cookbook, then left me alone to mix up the dough. We put the first pan of cookies in the oven and watched them through the oven door window. Those cookies puffed up like mutant mushrooms, miniature atomic clouds. Mom reviewed with me what I had put in the cookies, and instead of 1 tsp baking soda, I had put in one cup. We threw away the rest of the dough, but did keep the baked cookies around for a while. Even though they were inedible, they were quite spectacular to look at. Little did I know those cookies were a harbinger of things to come.

The avocado garlic soup recipe admonished me to not be scared off by the enormous quantity of garlic in the soup. The cookbook author promised that slow simmering would mellow the garlic into a rich undertone accenting the flavor of the avocado. The reality was, no amount of simmering, or even cremation, was going to tame that gargantuan quantity of garlic. After consuming a few spoonfuls of that green liquid, I could wilt plants at twenty paces with my breath.

The quesidillas I made were not exactly a culinary disaster, they were more a cultural disappointment. I had moved back to Minneapolis after several years in Southern California, and I was eager to show everyone what I had learned on the West Coast. When I was invited to a potluck, I decided to wow everyone with my homemade flour tortillas, served warm with melted cheese.

After going through the potluck line, I chose a seat next to a guy who had a slice of quesidilla on his plate. He took a bite of the concoction, chewed on it thoughtfully, then said, "You know, this store-bought lefse never tastes as good as the homemade stuff."

Not all of my cooking disasters have occurred in the distant past. A week or so ago, I was leafing through a cookbook, looking for chicken recipes, looking for something I hadn't made before. The Peking Chicken caught my eye. Granted, chicken didn't impart the same glamour to the recipe as duck, but I had chicken in the refrigerator, and so I decided to give it a try. The recipe stated it is traditional to serve the Peking Duck/Chicken sliced, then rolled up in mandarin pancakes with a special sauce, green onions and cilantro. Somewhere in the back of my mind I vaguely remembered that mandarin pancakes were a lot like crepes. The recipe suggested using flour tortillas as a substitute, but flour tortillas seemed too thick for this. I had lefse in the refrigerator, and decided to use it instead. I carefully wrapped a stack of lefse sheets in foil and put them in the oven to warm, as the recipe instructed. When it came time to eat, I unwrapped the foil and found a moist glob of dough that refused to be separated into sheets again.

Green Rice, a major diaster of my teenage years was the direct result of my gastronomic innocence, when I believed that if a recipe was in print, it couldn't be wrong. The enormous quantity of dried parsley called for in the recipe would have shocked an experienced cook, but trusting soul that I was, I made it exactly as the recipe was written. At dinner that night, I had to endure the smirking comments of my younger brother, who asked if I had used all the grass clippings from the freshly mowed lawn in my dish. (Please note, brother, now that this incident has been made public, it can no longer be used for blackmail purposes!)

When I moved to Park Rapids, I was delighted to discover a patch of wild blackberries next to my garage. I decided to make a blackberry pie and searched my cookbooks for recipes. All I could find was an apple and blackberry pie that was mostly apples, so, foolhardy soul that I am, I decided to improvise and use a recipe for blueberry pie as a guide. When the pie came out of the oven it looked and smelled wonderful, and I could hardly wait to taste it. When I did bite into a piece, I discovered an important difference between blueberries and blackberries. Blackberries have an attitude—woody seeds and a big, tough core. Trying to eat a bite of that pie was like chewing on flavored fiberboard.

Undaunted, I decided to try a different blackberry dessert. The blackberry tart recipe had directions on how to cook the berrries, then strain out the seeds and core before making the filling. The filling tasted great, and I knew this was going to be the ultimate blackberry dessert. The final step before baking was to use a pastry tube to squeeze out a soft dough on top of the filling for a lattice crust. I put the final flourish on the crust, and the whole thing sank out of sight. It stubbornly refused to resurface in spite of my many efforts at rescue and I ended up baking it as it was. Slices of the tart revealed long twisting snakes of crust, now a brilliant purple, embedded in the filling, and the recipe was renamed "Purple Worm Tart."

On another occasion, my aunt in California had sent me a large box of fresh dates. After eating a considerable amount plain, I decided to try cooking with them. The date nut bread was good, and so were the date-filled cookies. Never having learned when to leave well enough alone, I went in search of more date recipes, and found a recipe for Chinese Eight Treasure Dessert. Dates were one of the eight treasures in the dessert, and so were candied cherries and honey; the main ingredient, however, was lotus seeds. If lotus seeds were not available, the recipe advised canned garbanzo beans could be substituted. I was intrigued, and I had a relapse into my strange-ingredient phase. I made the recipe with garbanzos, and I must admit it did look unusual. My husband eyed the strange looking melange, and being a good sport did eat a few bites. His Minnesota nice comment was, "You probably don't need to save the recipe."

I could avoid a lot of future cooking disasters by only sticking with tried and true take-out, but there's no fun in that. Instead, I think I'll just hang a sign in my kitchen, *Caveat Gustator* , Eater Beware.

Charlie Bucker

"A perfect disgrace."
"An absolute eyesore!"
Click - click - click - click - click

So, that was it! A great mystery had just been solved for Charlie Bucker. Braced on one of his two garbage cans, he leaned forward to peer through an opening in the row of lilac bushes that screened his yard from snooping neighbors. When the high-heeled vision of the Anderson twins disappeared into the corner apartment building, Charlie spat an outraged spit. The insults so outweighed the chronic grind in his hip that he barely limped as he hurried along the tilting boardwalk to the front stoop. The muscles in his chin trembled less than an inch below the tip of his nose. "I'll perfect disgrace 'em...I'll give 'em eyesores!" He tore a curl of paint from the siding. He threw it to the porch floor and pounded it to powder in a furious little jig.

Making a leap forward to avoid catching the heel of his slipper, he let the screen door slam. A few minutes later, a black snake of coffee, made at five that morning and reheated twice by ten, spiraled from the spout of a tin percolator. His tail bone cut painfully into the remaining fibers of his butt muscles, as he bounced the chair closer to the table. He tilted backwards, to a dangerous angle, in order to check the front window. "Damn old hens!" Charlie growled. "So jealous they can't see straight."

The mystery Charlie solved out front concerned a sign tacked to his porch railing. It was written in red ink on the back of a punch-out from a Kleenex box. "Clean up your act," it read. Staring at the words again, he swung his cup in the general direction of his mouth, adding amoeboid patterns to his plaid shirt front.

"Flustrated old maids! I should just go over there right now. I ought to just bust right in and give 'em a shot of what they haven't had all these years!"

He pushed from the table, hitched up his shapeless trousers and paced out the remained of a lewd, vengeful fantasy.

The cliché of a man's home being his castle was a living creed for Charlie Bucker. He had wrung out a life for thirty years in this one-story, four-room bungalow. He worked six days a week for twenty-eight years at the OK Inn, until he had saved enough to buy the house outright. One Saturday, he saw the "For Sale" sign. On Sunday, he knocked on the door and asked the price. Monday morning, he paid the owner from a brown paper bag packed with tens and twenties. The next Sunday, he moved in with his scanty collection of worldly belongings. Later that year, his ancient mother joined him, lived a few tremulous months, then left him all she owned. A fingerful of wire hangers, on which a half-dozen withered dresses hung, still haunted a small closet off the pantry.

In recent times, arthritis stopped Charlie from curing the acne that curled paint shards from the house's exterior and dropped a lacy border of chips around the foundation. The interior, except for an amber glaze from his non-stop pipe-smoking, was well cared for. His furnishings were sparse, every item having had to pass the Charlie Bucker Test: "What's it good for?" His one extravagance was a pair of castanets that hung from a nail above the sink. The name, "Teresa," sang across his mind whenever he looked at them. His mother's clothes and the stilled noise-makers were the old man's only non-utilitarian objects—companions—in the silent house.

"Fat-kneed heifers!" he grunted, recalling the morning's insults. Charlie was sure those twins would sell their souls to live in a genuine home, instead of having to crawl inside the guts of a brick giant every day. Everyone in that mean neighborhood was jealous. How else to explain the pointing and laughing, the standard rhyme for "Bucker" scrawled on his garbage cans and the planks in his walkway...signs tacked to the rail? Those two look-a-likes, they did it. Just the types to have red ink. He saw them in his imagination—pens held like daggers—stalking the night—sneaking toward Charlie's porch. Snakes in the grass!

An oval was cut from a tablet-back. A hunt through a drawer under the sink produced a yellow pencil. Sitting at the newly caffeine-puddled table, Charlie began his labors. The greater part of the "labor" involved not biting clear through his tongue while controlling the shimmy in his writing hand. The message read, "Mind your own business you nosy snakes." He slid his bunions into a pair of "Romeo" slippers, picked up the terrible oval and a long carpet tack, and headed outdoors to wreak vengeance on the Anderson twins.

As happened countless times before, his courage lost its cutting edge when he reached the lilac hedge. He groaned several times, then lifted the lid of the nearest rubbish can. The cardboard slid down a pile of similar messages inside. Charlie had never yet delivered one of his outcries to insulters, but there was a balm in the writing of them.

In realigning the trash cans, something unfamiliar caught his eye. He thought it was a rat, at first, then realized it was a tiny rabbit. Charlie squatted, stroked its head with one finger. The gentle stroking parted the creature's ears and they dropped to the sides of the small body. The old man's face was only inches away as he whispered the first words of love he had uttered in five decades. Charlie got to his feet and hurried to the house. As he padded the inside of a mixing bowl with scraps of flannel from his rag bag, he decided to name the rabbit "Tess," be it boy or girl. He felt a heartbeat in his throat as he scuffed back to the front yard.

Nothing! An empty hollow in the ground. He moved both metal can, upsetting one of them, then grunted to his knees and crawled along the wall of lilacs. Still on his hands and knees, Charlie moved to the street side of the bushes. The spiky prongs of his elbows supported him for a moment before his face touched the ground. The dizzy spell seemed anchored somewhere under his breastbone. His cry bent and parted the blades of grass. "Come back," he moaned. "Oh, please...come back!"

"You've been awful nice to me," Charlie said, straightening in his chair and adjusting the sweater that had just been laid across his shoulders.

"Don't you be silly, Mr. Bucker," a woman's voice scolded. "You know you would have done the same for us."

"Why, of course," the second woman said.

"I don't know what happened to me out there."

"You lost your bunny rabbit—that's what you said." The voice was filled with sympathy.

"And don't worry about the trash," the second voice insisted. "We picked up all those papers and put the lid back on."

"I thank you for that," Charlie said, realizing anew that he had passed out in the yard.

"What was your bunny's name?"

"Tess."

"Aw...and was it a long-time companion?"

"No-time," the old man whispered, "...just found her today."

"And you called her Tess already?"

"It's a pet name," Charlie responded.

Struggling to produce long-unused hospitable tones, he asked, "How did you know my name?"

With a dozen apologies, and with pleas for understanding, the women explained that they couldn't help seeing his name on envelopes as they picked up the spilled debris from the overturned trash can. On hearing that, the morning's insult crashed back into Charlie's brain.

"Why, Mr. Bucker...are you all right?"

"You're not feeling dizzy again, are you?"

"I'm fine," Charlie snapped, suddenly struck by an idea. "Just remembered something. I've got to write it down. Either of you got a pen?"

In what was obviously a traditional purse-searching ritual, both women emptied the contents onto their laps.

"Here we go," one twin said.

"No, use mine," said the other. "I just filled it last night."

"Red ink?" asked the squinting man.

"Red? Good heavens! What kind of tramps do you think we..."

Silence thudded down on the threesome like an immense boulder. Charlie covered his face with both hands. The twins looked at each other meaningfully.

"Mr. Bucker, we know what you're thinking."

"Mr. Bucker, did you believe we wrote that 'clean up your act' message?"

"Mr. Bucker, we have never done anything so rude in our lives."

An incensed "Mr. Bucker!" concluded their protest.

Convinced that he had been wrong about the twins being the perpetrators, Charlie asked pardon for ever having such a thought. He said "I'm sorry" so many times that the women threatened to leave if he didn't stop. He finally did stop, but not before persuading them to call him Charlie, not Mr. Bucker.

A lengthy pause ensued, during which the visitors pivoted on their spiked heels and surveyed the room.

"My goodness, Mr. Bucker..."

"We mean 'Charlie,'" the other twin corrected.

"Yes, Charlie," the first twin said. "My goodness, what a charming little place you have. Charming! From the outside, a person wouldn't..."

"It's my castle," the old man beamed.

During the next pause, the women exchanged sidelong glances while Charlie dug into the dust-covered lobes of his brain in search of something polite to say. He leaned forward and slapped his knees when the excavation finally paid off.

"I'm just a regular fool, I guess. I don't even know you girls' names."

"I'm Marlyss Anderson," said one twin.

"I'm Mavis," said the other.

Then two forefingers, in a perfectly synchronized movement, shot forward and twisted against the seated man's plaid shirt front.

"...But you can call us 'Nosy' and 'Snaky.'"

They clasped each other in a hiccuping siege of laughter.

Charlie shoulder-bounced the sweater off, wrestled to his feet and made a bee-line for the coffee pot. As he put a match to the burner, he pointed to a shelf over the sink. A moment later, three cups rattled in their saucers as the laughing duet turned into a table-shaking trio.

Not much later, Marlyss stood at the sink, refilling the coffee pot. Mavis lifted the castanets from their nail and turned to Charlie.

"You play these?" she asked.

The old man's mouth fell open. He shook his head, no.

"Do you?" Charlie asked. "...Play them?"

Slipping the cords over her thumb and finger, she replied, "Hold on to your sombrero, señor."

Marlyss began humming the "Habanera" from *Carmen,* and a scene unfolded in the ballroom of Charlie's castle that would have very much surprised Mr. Bucker's nosy neighbors. Soon he was clapping to the rhythm while his shaggy slippers beat a tattoo on the hardwood floor. Every few measures, he shouted *Ole!,* cheered to his powdery old marrow by the understanding that his thirty-year sentence to solitary confinement was now past.

Roberta Palmer

Just Me

I have come of age.
Age of discovery,
Old age,
Middle age,
My age—Now.

I look back to pull some
idea of—Why?
But it's a joke.
Life is life,
something more,
something less,
or nothing!!

Life is just that—Life.
The age of living.

Pushed out of the womb,
to participate in life.
Wait for a
pat on the back,
shake of the hand,
or a smile.

To live in a
world of Dead Minds,
wanting to become rich and
powerful;
as assessment of their strengths.
Ignorant of anything
beyond the shell.

I've been a child, a teen,
young adult, model, student, nurse,
educator, teacher, helper, mentor.
A friend, Mother, sister, daughter,
mature.

Now I am me.

I have loved, hated,
remembered, forgot.
Been angered, hurt,
frustrated, and inspired.

Heart beating strong.
Wait!! Can we do more
than the part
we are assigned?

Correct me if I'm wrong,
am I still but me?

Indiscriminate Eater

F ood is pagan. Nut-brown chapatis wrap slivers of carrots and tangy green onions in sticky rice. At first bite, an aromatic ginger, garlic and cardamon sauce streams down my chin.

I peel a steaming, earthy cornhusk, and bite into salty masa to pursue the racy pleasure of red chillies and shredded pork tamales leaping in my mouth.

I munch a crunchy-crisp egg roll. Hot Chinese mustard strikes the taste buds on my tongue, and a warrior's tears wet my cheeks.

Food draws me into a juicy world, perfumed by compounds so attuned to my nature that I taste a succulent, sun-ripened peach before I bite into it.

Food captures my soul, and I fall headlong into a multitudinous universe. Red peppers, yellow peppers, black, blue and true green peppers marinated in a tangy tarragon and olive-oil vinaigrette and sprinkled with crushed black pepper; white crisp onion rings, simultaneously sweet and biting, incite me to follow the bongo beat of their call.

Soul is seduced shamelessly by my mother's double-crust, granny-smith apple pie. A crisp, lard-laden pie crust, dusted with cinnamon and sugar, envelops a generous pie tin of apple slices macerated in tantalizing caramel.

Soul is always losing its way. Delectable Atlantic oysters, topped with spinach sauteed in garlic and butter and baked until the tip of the oyster curls in its pearly shell, lead me on to the complex flavors of Steak Diane and crunchy, spring-green Romaine lettuce showered in Parmesan cheese and flavored by pressed, pungent garlic and red-wine vinegar.

Soul revels in misery, and is wracked with addictions. Waffles baked to a toasty brown floating in butter and ambrosial maple syrup. My mother's Swedish cinnamon rolls allure me with smells of sugar and cinnamon, and their sticky, sweet taste. "Don't stuff yourself." "One half of a cinnamon roll can't hurt you." "Take only enough to get a taste." "Why do you always overeat?"

Food links us with our childhood and pulls us back and back to times still desperate and full of meaning. Creamy, rose-tinted Campbell's tomato soup; salty oyster crackers float like alligators, partially submerged. Dad urges me to swallow, saying, "Hot soup heals a sore throat."

Torrents of tears and anger mark my crumpled face. Mother comforts me with a plate of sour cream, sugar cookies.

And we cook...burgundy globes of glossy eggplant, sliced and salted. Bitter juices drip and pool under the rack. Pat dry with a paper towel and dip twice. First in egg diluted with milk, and secondly, finely crushed Saltine crackers blended with Italian herb-seasoned flour. Heat olive oil to a sizzle in a ponderous black-iron skillet. Brown quickly, reduce the flame, and bake 5 minutes until your mouth and eggplant feel as one.

And we cook...Basmanti rice, long grain, white, fragrant rice. Rinse, drain, and pour cold water above the rice as high as the second knuckle on your middle finger. Cover and simmer gently for 20 minutes.

And we cook...salad greens are washed and trimmed. Mix together butter lettuce, red-leaf lettuce, romaine, arugula, endive, fresh spinach. Slice golden-ripe pome pears over a mound of blue cheese and top with toasted pine-nuts. Drizzle the pears with red-wine vinegar, honey and safflower oil dressing.

In pursuit of pagan pleasures, must I taste and eat everything? " I never know what is enough until I know what is more than enough."

Posole

1 to 2 chipotle peppers
2 tablespoons vegetable oil
1 medium onion, diced
1 red bell pepper (or green) chopped
1 small zucchini, diced
1 large tomato, cored and diced
2 cloves garlic, minced
2 cups hominy, yellow or white, cooked
1 cup cooked pink beans*, drained and rinsed (*pinto or cranberry beans)
3 cups water or vegetable stock
2 1/2 tablespoons tomato paste
2 teaspoons paprika
1 1/2 teaspoons dried oregano
1/2 teaspoons ground black pepper
1/2 teaspoons salt

Soak the chipotle in warm water for 30 minutes. Drain the liquid, remove the seeds, and mince.
Heat the oil in a large saucepan and add the vegetables, garlic and chipotle. Saute for 6 to 8 minutes, until the vegetables are tender. Add the hominy, beans, water, tomato paste and seasonings and simmer for 45 minutes to 1 hour, stirring occasionally.
Ladle the posole into soup bowls and serve with warm tortillas.

ᵇATTER UP

ᵇLOCK PRINT

Jamie Juntti

Meghan Strom

My Grandma's Kitchen

All the grandkids got a chance to sleep over at Grandma's. I was special because I only came down to Minnesota in the summer. On warm nights, she'd tuck me into bed up in my mom's old bedroom and read stories from the old *Uncle Remus* book. The binding was cracked, and some of the pages were loose, tattered and stained from Grandma's five children and umpteen grandchildren's sticky fingers who had heard the stories before me. The words on those yellowing pages came to live when Grandma read the stories of B'rer Rabbit and the Tar Baby.

In the morning, my face would be warm from the sun streaming through the thin, white curtains. I'd go downstairs, and Grandma would have breakfast ready; she'd already been up for a few hours. After breakfast, we'd set to work at our jobs for the day. Sometimes we'd weed the garden, or I would scrub the bird bath or pick the currants to make pies. Some days, one of my aunts or my mother would come over to butcher the chickens or freeze sweet corn, but my favorite task was when we made cookies together.

Cookies were an important part of Grandma's house. When you entered the house through the kitchen door, as we all did, your first stop would be at the two Tupperware containers on the counter behind the door. The two containers, one rectangular and one square, both with soft, pliable lids, were always filled with cookies. Graham crackers with white and chocolate icing between them are my Uncle Denny's favorite. Raisin-filled cookies that appeared around the Christmas holidays were my mom and Aunt Jo's favorite. Many of my cousins loved the chewy raisin or chocolate chip oatmeal cookies. Since my Grandma was a survivor of the Great Depression, she always made positively sure that each cookie had *only one* chocolate chip.

I enjoyed all of these, but when I came to Grandma's, we made sugar cookies. Grandma would send me to get old sections of the newspaper, and we'd spread them out over the entire counter where we worked. This, she explained, would make cleaning up a lot quicker and easier. Out of her recipe box, Grandma would find the recipe for sugar cookies; it was spattered with cookie dough. She clipped the recipe into the beak of a little bird fashioned out of a clothes pin made just for the job of holding the recipe. I would pull the tall mint-green stool over to the counter, and wait expectantly for her to hoist me up onto it, knowing full well she wouldn't until she sent me to the sink to wash my hands. When my hands were clean, she would give me a boost up onto the kitchen stool, and we would finally begin.

Grandma would lift her large, yellow mixing bowl down from the cupboard over my head and place it in front of me. With dented, tin measuring cups, I would measure out twice the amount of every ingredient in the recipe. She helped me use the flat side of a knife to level off all the measurements. We had to double it to make sure she wouldn't run out too soon. Grandma would help me add the sugar and butter and by then I would already be antincipating the sweet taste of the cookies. Grandma would get out a little bowl. One at a time I would crack brown-shelled eggs bought from her neighbor, into the little bowl so I could fish out all the bits of eggshell before they could make their way into our cookies. With the aluminum measuring spoons, I measured out 2 teaspoons of nutmeg and dropped them into the bowl, and appetizing warm smell of spice filled my nose. Before the mixture became too thick, I would stir it with a large wooden spoon. Then I continued to add lemon extract and baking soda in sweet milk. Grandma would usually mention how she didn't know how they got anything right on the cooking shows on TV, because they'd throw a pinch of this or a handful of that, willy-nilly wihtout ever measuring. Next came the job of sifting the flour. Grandma would bring out a large container of flour from the cupboard directly below me. With an old-fashioned sifter, I sifted seven cups of flour into a bowl. We added the flour and carefully measured the remaining ingredients, two teaspooons of baking powder and a half teaspoon of salt. I would wrap my small arm around the mixing bowl and try to stir through the thick mixture. I would stir with both my right, them my left hand and then both together until my five year old arms were too tired. Grandma would finish the job in what seemed to be a few effortless moments.

When the dough was all mixed, I would hop down off my perch on the the stool at the level of the counter and dash across the kitchen to the cupboard where the glasses were kept, eager to stamp out the cookies. Grandma would gently explain that we had to put the dough into the fridge for an hour before making it into cookies so it would firm up and not be runny or crumbly. She would roll the dough into a large ball in the bottom of the big yellow bowl and carefully hand it to me. Reluctantly I would carry the bowl over to the fridge and place it on the shelf that Grandma had cleared. The hour long wait until we could roll out and start baking the cookies was usually a little nerve-wracking. We would clean up the area we worked in by rolling up and throwing out the top layer of newspaper that we had placed under our work surface. Grandma would fill a dish pan with warm water and foamy soap bubbles and pull my stool over to the sink. She would wash each cup, bowl and spoon and I dried them with the dish towel that she had embroidered with colorful little pictures of the days of the week, kittens or girls in sunbonnets.

When all the tasks in the kitchen were done, Grandma would send me down the short gravel road to the mailbox and I would pick up all the letters and the daily paper and bring them back to the house. Usually I had just enough time to skim over the cartoon pictures in the funnies before Grandma called me back into the kitchen. I would dash excitedly into the kitchen, wash my hands without hesitation and pull the stool back over to the counter. Sitting on the fresh layer of newspaper was the big yellow bowl full of dough, 2 cookie sheets, a dish of sugar and the most important tool, a small juice glass whose bottom was intricately cut-glass in a delicate pattern with scallops and curlicues which served as our cookie press. Grandma would roll little balls of dough and position them on the cookie sheet. I dipped the bottom of the glass in the little dish of sugar and stamped each little ball of dough into a flat, round cookie. Each cookie glistened with the little sugar crystals in the ridges of the design transferred from the bottom of the glass. When the cookie sheets were full, we moved them into the warm gas over that Grandma had lit with a long Strike Anywhere match.

When the first batch came out of the oven, the smell of warm, sweet cookies flooded the room. Grandma would hold the cookie sheet with a crocheted oven mitt, and slide the golden cookies onto yet another clean section of newspaper to cool. She often reminded me, "It is a poor cookie that doesn't grease its own pan." Like magic, the kitchen door would rattle open and in would walk various uncles and cousins who seemed able to sense that a fresh batch of Grandma's cookies had just been made. They were wearing farming clothes which had an almost pleasant smell of motor oil about them. They, too, were sent to the sink to wash before coming near the cookies. When they each ate their first, second, third and fourth cookie, I would beam with delight and pride, knowing I had a hand in making Grandma's well-loved cookies.

Happy conversation rang through the house while cups of coffee and cookies were downed. Slowly, the kitchen would empty again, and all that was left was Grandma, me and the remainder of the cookies. Grandma would get her fancy silver tray down which looked like it should be saved for special occasions. On it, she would arrange a generous amount of cookies. We poured two tall glasses of cold milk. Then Grandma and I would go into the dining room, sit side by side, and enjoy the cookies we made. We laughed and talked and filled our stomachs with sweet, delicious warmth that could only come from Grandma's kitchen.

Grandma's Sugar Cookies

1 cup white sugar
1 cup butter or shortening
2 eggs
1 teaspoon nutmeg
1 teaspoon lemon extract
1 teaspoon soda in 3 tablespoons sweet milk
3 1/2 cups flour
1 teaspoon baking powder
1/4 teaspoon salt

Mix above ingredients and roll into balls. Press with sugar-coated cookie press, or juice glass. Bake in a 350 degree oven for about 5 to 7 minutes or until the edges of cookies are firm and bottoms are lightly browned.

Revealed

peeling apples
in my kitchen
watching the jewel-red
circular stripes
falling away
from the edge of my paring
knife
revealing the firm white flesh
beneath

reminds me
of how
with sure fingers
you uncovered me
and took away my shyness
and insecurities
along with my clothes
and revealed the real me
naked, clean
and trembling
ready for the first heart-
stopping touch
of your lips...

Food for the Soul
#2 — At Table

I take my portion from the Cup.
The red stain
of a single drop
spreads upon my clothing.

Will evidence
of presence in His Presence
disappear as quickly
from the fabric of my faith
as from my wash and wear garment?

Grandma Erna's Kitchen

The memories of Grandma Erna's kitchen
float richly through my mind
banana bread, jams, yams and the best lefse you could find!
Hot dish, sweet corn, pickled beets and Swedish meatballs that make your mouth water
fresh raspberries over fluffy angel food cake
and polt sliced and fried in butter.

I have never tasted a taco, I think maybe I should,
she giggled at 79
I have never used store-bought spaghetti sauce, do you think it is any good?
she questioned at 89

The memories of Grandma Erna's table rest neatly in my mind
perfect linens, beautiful napkins several kinds
peanuts, mints, toffee, ruby glistening dish always tempting
come over morning or night
Your belly would never be empty.

We used to butcher a hog in a day, and pack it in hot lard
we kept it in a 30-gallon crock, right out in the yard.
For supper meat, reach right in
months and months it stayed good,
just remember to put the lid back on,
a brick on top of wood.

The memories of Grandma Erna's wisdom is sharp as a tack in my mind
she talked about the many things on which a person should dine.
What are you doing picking off that chicken skin?
I believe in being healthy
hearty, rosy
no one likes you too thin!

Ice cream before bed helps you to sleep hard,
if you're worried about fat, think about
eating a sandwich made of lard!
It is breakfast, lunch, dinner, coffee and then supper...get it right.
Dinner is served in the afternoon
supper is always at night!

Jenny Field

The memories of Grandma Erna's kitchen
float richly through my mind
banana bread, jams, yams and the best lefse you could find!
Hotdish, sweet corn, pickled beets and Swedish meatballs that make your mouth water
fresh raspberries over fluffy angel food cake
and polt sliced and fried in butter.

ⁱCE [¢]REAM [¢]ONE
^bLOCK PRINT

Sarah West

71

Shannon Geisen

Don't See the Stop Signs

I admit it.
I'm no Amelia Earhart of cuisine
flying solo over gourmet waters.

If a recipe calls for a teaspoon of ground cloves,
I measure carefully.

I pre-heat the oven to 375° when instructed.

I don't dice when I'm told to chop.

I always refrigerate salad dressing, peanut butter
and pancake syrup after opening the bottle —
            that's what you're supposed to do.

The recipe card box is tidy and cute,
with flowers stenciled in china blue.
It's filled with pasta, hamburger and tomato dishes.
In perfect penmanship.

There is order in my kitchen.
But I've broken a few traffic laws.
I don't wear a seatbelt.

I'm near-sighted, but
about a half-dozen times or more,
I drove my car without my glasses.
A bit of blindness proved enlightening.

Couldn't read the stop signs.

Decided not to yield.

Refused to make a u-turn.

Only saw green, for go, go, go.

Swimming in blurry images, everything
became a French Impressionist painting—all pastels and splotchy,
but beautiful.

No one could tell me where to go.

Now I always leave home
without a map.

^STRAWBERRY [¢]HECKERS
^BLOCK PRINT

Jeremy Lustila

Bridges

A crooked river mile downstream from an old wooden bridge, our canoe noses softly against the bank. Floating high and empty, it spins lightly on the slow current and points upriver, tugging gently at its tie rope. It's still early on this September morning, and we stand on the riverbank, shivering occasionally until the sun strengthens, soaking us in its warmth. Rose and I smile at each other as we pick highbush cranberries, which fall plop, ploppity into pails at our feet. Together we feel the familiar joy found in this timeless ritual, harvesting nature's bounty.

These fat rubies hang translucent in the soft morning light. Round and full with a tough skin which pops audibly in our mouths, their tart interior puckers our faces and reminds me of the little crab apples I picked in the neighbor's yard when I was a kid. The rich, sharp smell of this moist lowland habitat has a peculiar tang all its own, and is a prominent part of its flavor. When we have picked everything in reach, we reload the canoe and drift downriver, searching for the next bush.

We scan the riverbank ahead, looking for the telltale clumps of berries, hanging brilliant red and shiny in the sea of green. Some clumps are yellowish-orange and we pass them up, holding out for the fully ripe red berries. At each stop we fill the small pails hanging from our belts and empty them into the buckets waiting in our canoe.

Drifting downstream today, we both feel a special sense of contentment. This feeling cannot be quantified in a scientific manner, but it can be felt surrounding us. You could not be alive here, today, and not feel it. Even our canoe seems affected as it floats easily, parting the slow current with muted ripples. Fullness rises out of the ground like an invisible mist, warming our souls the way the sun warms our bodies. We have given ourselves to the land for this day, and are blessed by being part of the land and water around us. It is as natural for us to be here as the turtle basking in the sun or the sparrow flitting from bush to bush ahead of us.

We yield to the river, which carries us along at its own pace, heedless of any commitments we might have. The same speed for all that might use it. Picking berries allows Rose and me to reconnect to a richness often missing in our daily living. It is more than just the berries. It is the small act of spiritual healing which overshadows any harvest we might gather in our buckets that brings us here.

Rose and I go ashore in early afternoon for a lunch break. We sip coffee from the thermos as we laze on the ground, watching the current slip around our canoe. Two five-gallon buckets stand upright, overflowing with red berries, representing a bounty we'll enjoy for months to come. I wonder if those who have never tasted highbush cranberry syrup on sourdough pancakes, or sniffed the delicate bouquet of cranberry cordial, could really identify with the sense of wealth we feel, represented by those two buckets. Even if we didn't pick another berry, we would go home satisfied.

The heat is summer-like in its intensity and the river beckons invitingly. We yield willingly and strip before sliding naked into the water. Entering the water is like penetrating a membrane and I think of big soap bubbles, which let my finger pass nearly all the way through without disturbing the bubble itself. The river feels cool and fresh to us after the mid-day heat, softly tingling on our skin as we submerge. Except for our gentle splashing, it is quiet and I realize that it has been quiet all day. Many songbirds have already migrated southward, and the forest no longer rings with their calls. The warmth of the day rouses a few insects, but even they drone in a subdued manner. We let the current buoy us up as we lie fish-belly white in the shallow water, so languid and serene that it almost hurts when we have to abandon the river to make our way home.

Early in the morning we shuttled our vehicles so we could avoid paddling upstream at the end of the day. The whole operation had been tinged with a frantic sense of urgency that disappeared the moment the river grasped our canoe and began carrying us to the Gulf of Mexico. Now we paddle silently and I wonder what we will bring home after we take the canoe out and tie it on top of the car.

How long will the spirit of this day last? Will we remember the warm sun and the cool water long after the sinuous riverbanks are clothed in a blanket of white? Will the spirit of the land extend its peaceful harmony into our harried lives? When we crack open a jug of cordial, a memento from this day, will we taste again the sunny peace of this better world?

Wild Berry Cordial

This is the same recipe Rose and I used to make cordial from the highbush cranberries we picked while floating down the river. We have also used wild grapes and wild raspberries with very good success. We usually make a double batch.

It is normal to find a layer of pulpy sediment on the bottom of the bottles after they have been allowed to sit quietly for a while. This is very drinkable and does not affect the flavor. It will not look as pretty in the glass when you drink it. This cordial is very good on ice and probably on ice cream as well.

We save the vodka bottles and use them for bottling the cordial. You can use any type of bottle or canning jar. We wash our bottles and jars, and rinse them with boiling water to sterilize them before bottling the cordial. By storing the bottled cordial out of direct sunlight and avoiding extremes in temperature we have kept it for two years with no problems. When we make cordial in late summer and early fall we plan on opening it around Thanksgiving. The original recipe recommends aging at least two to three weeks. Longer aging seems to improve the flavor. It can be stored in the refrigerator after it is opened if you desire.

Day 1. Mash 3 quarts of berries. Cover them and set in a cool place for 24 hours.

Day 2. Pour a fifth of vodka, (or 190 proof Everclear), into the mashed berries. Stir to mix and allow to sit in a cool place another 24 hours.

Day 3. Mix 3 cups of water with 6 cups of sugar and heat to boiling. Then chill this sugar syrup until it is very cold. While the syrup is cooling, strain the berry mix through a cheesecloth or jelly strainer to remove most of the seeds and pulp. When the syrup is cold, mix thoroughly with the berry liquor and bottle. There is no processing or canning involved. Remember this is for a single batch. Yield will vary due to the juice content of the berries.

Peppercorn Rhythm

A tiny fist on your tongue, a smoking eye, a dainty tidbit
roaring down a one-way street. One grain of howling heat.

A gargoyle gone mad, shark and gypsy, jaguar, a ghost spiraling in
your nose. The black sneeze, the scorpion bead, the grackle in your laugh.

When she sticks our her leg, you trip
descending, ascending—delicious she is—all sequin and spitfire.

Her shriveling dark licks your tongue to bright flame
and your mouth O's...

Her froth sizzles a prayer from your lips.
And on she rolls, an asterisk winking, a footnote burning.

She's old as Eden and satisfied to seat out your secrets,
knowing you have no idea what you'll tell
when all hell breaks loose in your mouth. And just when you think
you can take no more of her pungent, peppery beating, there's rain.

Peppercorn Kiss Steak

1/4 cup black peppercorns, cracked in a mortar with a pestle
2 beef tenderloin steaks. Cut from the center of the loin, 1 1/2 to 2 1/2-inches thick, and flatten with a mallet or cleaver
Sea salt
1 or 2 green onions, diced
1/4 pound butter
1/4 cup, plus 1 tablespoon brandy
1 to 2 tablespoons Grey Poupon Dijon mustard
1/4 to 1/2 cup half-and-half or heavy cream

Set up a charcoal grill. Season the steaks with sea salt, and press the cracked pepper onto both sides of the steaks. Set aside.

Saute the onion in butter, using a cast iron skillet on the stove or grill. Begin to grill the steaks, using some of the green onion and butter mixture for basting. Keep the remaining butter warm by placing the skillet on the side of the grill.

When the steaks are done, place them in the skillet with the green butter. Add the brandy carefully and flame. Move the steaks to one side of the skillet, and add the Grey Poupon and cream, stirring quickly to blend well.

Place the steaks on individual platters, and pour the mustard sauce over them. Serves two.

Author's Note: During a lazy summer several years ago, I discovered a description of Steak au Poivre in a sleazy novel. My husband and I adapted the recipe to our culinary skills, and it has become our anniversary specialty.

This is elegant dining. You will want to use your best dishes, and put on a romantic CD. Chunk or slice some melon (we prefer honey dew), slather it with lime juice and top it with a maraschino cherry to soften the bite of the peppercorn kiss. A lively salad and a cheesy potato are perfect companions to Peppercorn Kiss Steak. Bon appetit!

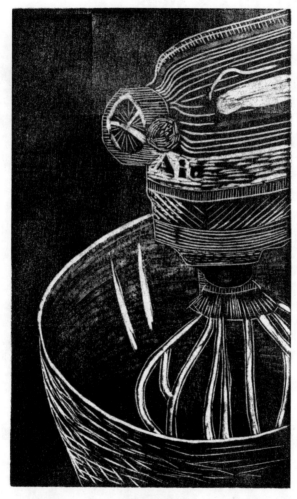

mIXER

WOOD ENGRAVING

Dawn Rossbach

Janet Pratt

Ode to My Refrigerator

I sent you away today
to get a fresh new look:
white, not avocado,
so you will not feel ugly
in my new blue and white kitchen

Tomorrow you'll be back in your corner
singing contentedly
as you store our treasures,
maintain our health
and preserve our daily bread

I'm aware of you more today
fonder, now that you are away
(Isn't that how it goes?)
And this time, I promise you can stay,
Old faithful hummer!

Jayson Knutson

the cookbook

I look through it,
  looking for a recipe,
the cookbook has so
    much good looking food,
I have a hard time to figure out,
  what to cook,
    the cookbook and I
always get along,
  too well,
    so I will go,
and cook it all,
if only I had the time to...

81

Penelope Swan

Remembering Mexico

Remembering Mexico
that breezy rooftop
restaurant in the Sierra Madres
our view of Liz T.'s mimosa tree
hugging and drinking and laughing for hours
we stay warm
not noticing food
has become an imaginary subject at our table

and our camerara virtuoso she
woos us. Croons. Winking and swinging
and bending low, teases a song over your shoulder.

This earthy dumpling fevers us
her voice sliding sultry. Silkily.
I have seen your food and it looks
delicious, she smoothes again and again

passing us by with plates plumped pink
with camerones and guacamole mountains
salsa limed cool and jalapeñoed hot

bottles and bottles of gleaming cerveza

luscious are we and so happy in another country
a glittery city spangling below. Above,
the dizzying violet dark
like this love poem
honey-mouthed
o p e n

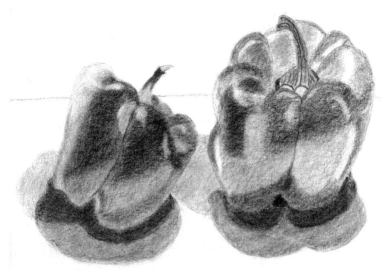

GREEN PEPPE^r
GRAPHITE ^dRAWING

Nancy J. Kocurek

Penelope Swan

Sassy Enough Fruit Salsa

1/2 to 1 cup each of fresh fruit: pineapple tidbits,
    kiwi tidbits, sliced strawberries
1 jalapeño pepper, finely diced
1/2 red bell pepper, diced
Juice of 1/2 lime
1/3 cup orange juice

Cut up the fruit, and toss lightly with the lime juice. Set aside.

Dice the peppers, being very careful not to touch face or eyes when dicing the jalapeño pepper. Add the pepper and the orange juice to the fruit, and toss gently. Cover and chill for one-half hour before serving. Best when not made too far in advance of serving. Excellent with ham. Serves 4 to 6 people.

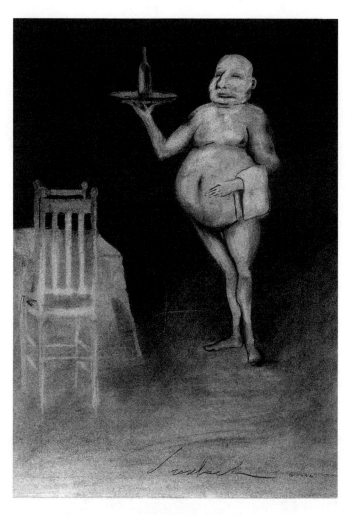

tHE nAKED WAITER
ᶜHARCOAL ᵈRAWING

Dawn Rossbach

The Food Critic

The filet of sole lay on the floor and beside it, the splendid Tomatsmor, the tomato butter Amber had fixed for Orval's supper. The white tablecloth she pressed so carefully earlier that day was half off the table and stained deep red by the glass of St. Louis Bougelleis. Amber held the only dish she'd managed to save from Orval's temper, the Lanttulaatikko, rutabaga casserole.

"Meat and potatoes," Orval growled. "Who do you think you're serving up here? You think you're opening up some high falutin' restaurant? Get me a steak and a potato."

She imagined the Lanttulaatikko sailing elegantly from her fingertips and landing on Orval's balding, fat head. But, of course, she knew she'd never do such a thing.

"I guess there is no point encouraging you to try something new, now that most of it is on the floor, is there?" she said and smiled. "I give you credit—you really know how to get your point across that you don't like fish."

"I don't like fish. I don't like tomatoes. I don't like rutabagas. I don't like wine," Orval said through crooked yellow teeth.

"It will take about forty-five minutes for the potato to cook," Amber told her husband of three years.

"I'll be watching the game in the den."

He got up, and she fully expected that he would knock the table over completely, with a wide swipe of his hand to finish the destruction he'd begun earlier. But he didn't and Amber left the mess, walked into the kitchen and pulled a single potato out of the bag, scrubbed it and put it into the oven. She took a steak from the freezer and popped it into the microwave.

The ingredients for her special meal still sat on the counter. Unrinsed pots and spoons were stacked up in the sink. Dots of whipped butter plastered the upper cabinets. The floor was sprinkled with nutmeg, salt, bits of dry bread.

Amber sat down on the stepping stool she used to reach high places since she was short, not even five feet. She picked up the stained cookbook, a few of its pages branded in the circles of her electric burners. It was a special cookbook she'd only recently rediscovered. Her sister brought it back some twenty years ago from a trip to Norway back before Astrid became hailed in New York as one of the finest French hornists in the Philharmonic.

Amber loved her sister—never in her life had she been envious of Astrid, or wished for her glamorous metropolitan life. Amber had been content to go to a small liberal arts college, graduate with a BA in art history and thought her life was set when she landed a nice job at the Minerva County courthouse processing licensing fees and property tax payments. The people she worked with were kind, maybe a little dull, but she didn't mind dullness. Every year she received two weeks paid vacation. That was her time when she'd visit Astrid in New York, or where ever Astrid was performing.

Shortly after Amber unceremoniously turned forty, Orval Anderson asked her out on a date. Amber had a simple quality to her features and while she was no raving beauty, inexplicably, she'd never been asked out on a date before then, not even in high school, and she was oblivious to the joys of being noticed by someone until Orval came along.

"Why can't you just live with him?" Astrid pleaded when Amber broke the news she was getting married. "He's just so—not your type."

"He's okay," Amber said pleasantly. "And he asked nicely. He got down on one knee."

"So?"

"It made an impression on me," Amber said.

"I don't think it's going to work out, but congratulations anyway." The two sisters had hugged and Amber was pleased that her sister approved.

The newlyweds lived in Amber's house; the one she'd purchased with money made investing on the stock market. Amber read the *Wall Street Journal* daily and habitually read books about investing. Sir Robert Churchill, the champion of mutual funds, was her hero. His book of *Daily Quotes; More Than Just Making Money*, lay on her nightstand and ritualistically she read five pages before falling asleep.

Orval didn't know about Amber's investments, not because she didn't tell him, but because she had gone into such detail, he couldn't comprehend what she meant by large caps and small caps or IPOs or capital gains. He gave her half of his paycheck every month from his job in Maintenance at the courthouse and ignored her rambling on about projected earnings and interest rates.

Sir Robert said in his book, "It is nice to be important, but it is more important to be nice." So Amber sat on the stool looking through the cookbook and wondered if maybe she should try one of the desserts. Orval didn't have strong feelings about desserts; at least he hadn't expressed any strong feelings about them in the years since they married in the judge's chamber. In fact, she remembered how much he enjoyed the small chocolate cake they had ordered for the wedding reception.

She decided on Hovdessert, meringues with chocolate sauce. The microwave signaled that the steak was probably thawed. Amber tossed the cookbook onto the cluttered counter and pulled a frying pan from the drawer below the oven. She put the steak in the pan and turned the stove to high, then returned to the cookbook and read the ingredients: egg whites, sugar, butter, flour, cocoa—all things she had on hand.

Getting out her biggest mixing bowl, she began cracking eggs, separating out the yolks. It took her several tries, but she was determined, enjoying the challenge of learning how to crack an egg with one hand.

"What the hell is burning?" Orval hollered.

The steak held down a billowing cloud of brown smoke. Amber casually turned the seared meat over and hollered back, "Something must have fallen under the burner. Everything is fine."

She rinsed off the beaters for the electric mixer, then started to whip the egg yolks. Amber refused to eat eggs when she was a child because the way they looked when they were raw. Transforming the thin, ghoulish membrane into stiff peaks of lovely white gave her a thrill equal to a five-point gain on the market. Or better yet, she thought to herself, it was like the excitement of selling one of her oil paintings for fifteen dollars at the local craft fair just the month before.

When they were first dating, Orval told her the painting of an orange in her living room was the finest picture he'd ever seen. "You oughta sells these at the County Arts and Crafts Fair," he'd complimented her. "Those guys must make a ton. My sister and her friends go every year when us guys go out hunting and they always come back with more junk."

His words had echoed in her mind for the past years and she was surprised at Orval's reaction when she showed him the money she'd made on the sale. "A two-year-old paints better than you. Whoever bought that piece of crap must have wanted to spruce up the outhouse."

"You goof-ball." Amber had given his shoulder a little punch and then thinking aloud, added, "I might use some of my investment money to go back to art school."

"I ain't never seen any of that fantasy money of yours—don't think you can come asking me for a loan. And don't you have to be at least a little bit talented to go to those places? They'd laugh you right out of the building."

"You're suppose to go to school to learn, not because you know everything. You're so thick," Amber teased him good-naturedly.

Orval didn't like being called thick. He had expressed his anger by ripping up her canvases, shredding the still-lifes and sunset studies she'd brought out to show him. What did it matter really, Amber thought afterward, admitting to herself as she threw away the remains, she didn't like the paintings much and knew it was a bit of a pipe dream. Serious artists all lived in Paris or New York and lived deep, passionate lives. Serious artists could talk about all the different art movements, the minimalist, the impressionist, the surrealist, and cubist. Her painting amounted to nothing more than the local Ben Franklin store getting a chance to sell their expensive tubes of oils that no one else in town would buy.

Smoke again filled the kitchen and Amber flipped the steak. It looked done to her. She poked at the potato in the oven with a fork—still hard. She took it out and plopped it into the microwave. Orval didn't like his potatoes microwaved, but Amber discovered he only didn't like it when he knew about it.

She returned to her meringues, dropping the foamy snowballs onto a cookie sheet. Orval came into the kitchen.

"Aren't you going to clean up this mess?" he asked.

"I'm making you a special dessert," Amber said and gave him her happy smile.

"What the hell is that?" he asked pointing at the white balls.

"Eggs."

"What did you do to it?"

"They're whipped," she said. Orval swiped one of the peaks with his finger and stuck it in his mouth. "They're still raw," Amber warned him.

He spat the foam onto the floor. "Dang, woman, that's disgusting."

"Well, they haven't baked yet and there is a sauce..."

Orval flung the meringue-covered cookie sheet up into the air where it bombed the cabinet doors, then clanged loudly to the floor.

"Where's my steak?" he barked. "Quit screwing around and get me my dinner."

"Coming right up," Amber said, pleased with her steady voice and cheerful tone. "Happiness pursued, eludes; happiness given, returns," Sir Robert's book instructed. "You go sit down and I'll bring it out to you. Do you want steak sauce?"

"I don't like steak sauce," Orval shouted in her face, spraying a fine, foul mist. Amber thought she heard his knuckles scraping the floor as he swaggered out of the kitchen.

She put the burned-up steak on a plate alongside the nuked potato. She poured Orval a tall glass of whole milk.

She enjoyed painting and had since girlhood. Astrid had several of Amber's paintings hung prominently in her New York apartment and she'd said that whenever she entertained, people always commented and asked about the artist. While Amber appreciated the compliments, she didn't believe a word of it. Still, Amber thought as she placed a sprig of parsley next to the steak and brought it out to Orval, even if no one else ever saw her creations, she enjoyed making them.

"You just don't hear good do you?" Orval shook his head. "I never realized how incredibly dense you are, woman." He took the parsley from his plate and dropped it on the floor. "I don't know what that weed is, but don't ever put it on my steak again, understand?"

That night, Amber cleaned the dining room and the kitchen. She threw away the white linen cloth and all the food. She threw away the dishes too. Another of Sir Robert's Daily Quotes came to mind: "Destructive language tends to produce destructive results."

"Orval," Amber sat down on the sofa in the den, next to Orval's Lazy Boy recliner. "I think I'd like to learn how to cook. I think I could be really good at it and have a lot of fun. Astrid says there are cooking schools...."

"Do I have to turn up the sound to get you to shut up?" Orval said, pointing the remote at his TV.

"Perhaps it would be best if you moved out and found someone else to make your steak. I don't really like making steaks." It felt so good to say it, but Amber was a little disappointed that he didn't hear her over the sports announcer.

Astrid called her the next night. "Paris for a month," she said excitedly. "Plan your vacation and come stay with me. The lodging is paid for and you can visit museums and be inspired by all sorts of wonderful things," Astrid tempted her.

"I wonder if Orval would notice," Amber mused to her sister. "I mean when he didn't get his steak and potato."

About a week later, they ate dinner off of paper plates. Fried chicken and mashed potatoes. "This leg tastes raw," Orval complained. "And these potatoes are barely mashed up. You're a lousy cook. Lousy painter, lousy housekeeper, especially a lousy cook." When he had eaten nearly every bite Amber felt positively giddy.

"Are you sure you don't want to move out Orval?" Amber asked politely. "I'd like to turn your room into a studio."

"What the hell would you be able to do in a studio? You're no good at anything. You can't even fry a frigging piece of chicken. Where the hell are the plates? You too lazy now to wash dishes?"

"I just don't think this marriage is much fun. I think a studio would be a better use for that bedroom is all I mean," Amber explained.

"It's not suppose to be fun," Orval hollered. "I'm not having fun either, but I don't complain. Now get me the damn ketchup." When Amber didn't respond right away, he punched a hole in the wall, causing her to jump up and run to the fridge.

After dinner, Amber hung one of her paintings over the hole.

While Orval watched TV, Amber read Tate Hauser's book *One Hundred W ays to Quiet Your Critic* . Hauser taught Creativity at a University in New Mexico where truly creative people lived and created beautiful homes and lived interesting lives and made enchanting things.

Orval went to bed at his usual time, ten sharp, like the military man he once was. She could hear his snores through his bedroom door. They never had shared a room. She was quiet and her calmness made her feel powerful. She opened the door slowly and looked around inside Orval's room and imagined the way the light would stream in through the southern window and shine on her easel.

Amber was counting on what Sue, who worked over at Births, Deaths, and Marriages, said about how easy a murder could be committed in their tiny county. The coroner was a family-practice man who only performed autopsies if there had been physical violence, a stabbing or shooting. All these heart attacks, her friend said, were probably poisonings or suffocation. "If there are no marks, how is an untrained person to know?" Sue had said.

Amber waited a little longer until she was sure that the half dozen sleeping pills she'd put in Orval's mashed potatoes had taken effect. Then gently putting the plastic bag that came with the Shake and Bake mix over his head, she twisted it and held it shut until he stopped sucking the plastic in and blowing it out. He never gave her any trouble, but just stopped breathing. "What a nice way to go," Amber thought to herself. "I hope that's how I die."

Astrid's hug was long and sympathetic. Several times during Amber's visit with her in Paris, Astrid remarked, "It's just so wonderful how you've handled your grief."

It was the classes at the Cordon Bleu though, that really changed Amber's life for good.

Tomatsmor Tomato Butter (Norwegian)

Makes 1/2 cup.

8 tablespoons unsalted butter (1 quarter-pound stick)
2 tablespoons tomato paste
1/2 teaspoon salt
1/4 teaspoon sugar

Cream the butter with an electric mixer set at medium speed or by beating it against the side of a bowl with a wooden spoon. When it is light and fluffy, beat in the tomato paste, salt, and sugar. Transfer to a serving bowl and chill until ready to serve. Serve cold, with hot grilled or fried fish.

Mrs. Richardson's Love Affair with Mr. Hershey Chocolate Cake

Oven 350°
2 nine inch cake pans, greased and lined with waxed paper
Baking time: 30 to 35 minutes.

8 (yes eight) bars of HERSHEY'S semi-sweet Baking Chocolate, broken into pieces
3 cups all purpose flour
1 1/2 cups sugar
2 teaspoons baking soda
1 teaspoon salt
2 cups water
2/3 cup vegetable oil
2 tablespoons white vinegar
2 teaspoons vanilla extract
1/2 jar Mrs. Richardson's Hot Fudge Topping

Melt chocolate in microwave at HIGH for 1 1/2 to 2 minutes or until chocolate is melted. Cool slightly.
In mixer bowl, combine the flour, sugar, baking soda, and salt. Add melted chocolate, water, oil, vinegar, and vanilla extract. Beat until thoroughly blended. Pour into prepared pans.
Bake. Cool completely. Frost between layers and top of cake with hot fudge topping that has been microwaved just long enough to spread on cake.
Serve with real sweetened whipped cream.

Turtle Cake Version: In addition to the hot fudge topping, drizzle your favorite caramel topping and sprinkle with toasted pecans in between and on top of layers.

A special thank you to the following businesses for their support in making it possible for the Jackpine Writers' Bloc to publish Volume # 9 of the *Talking Stick*.

Sponsor Level
Park Pharmacy - Park Rapids, MN
1st National Bank of Menahga - Menahga, MN
Park Rapids Enterprise- Park Rapids, MN

Benefactor Level
Wisconsin Telephone Association
Park Rapids/Walker Eye Clinic - Park Rapids, MN
Secret Garden - Park Rapids, MN
Bishops - Park Rapids, MN

Please send 6 hard copies of your submission for the next *Talking Stick*, which will be a literary journal, to Jackpine Writer's Bloc, P.O. Box 319, Menahga, MN 56464.

Colophon

The Talking Stick: A Literary Cookbook Issue, Volume 9, was published in May 2000 by the Jackpine Writers' Bloc. Dawn Rossbach designed the cover with Jennifer Sundrud's *Waldorf Salad.* Dawn Rossbach created the layout design with Atlantix Pro, Garamond, and Waif fonts, using Adobe PageMaker 6.0 on a Macintosh G3 and a Power Macintosh 7100/66. Assisting were Gail Gardner and Shannon Geisen. Artwork was prepared at Haas Printing. Haas Printing printed the book in Park Rapids, MN.